A man was standing at the rail, watching as the already overloaded lifeboat was being lowered. He was a big man, with strong well-cut features and responsible eyes. He was shaking his head and waving toward the boat as if telling them to go and leave him.

Then he turned and saw Gail, and exclaimed with horror that she was left behind. "Wait!" he shouted to the boat. "Here's a woman!"

"Too late!" she heard someone call. "Look! The ship! She's sinking!" And she felt a sensation as if the earth was about to sink beneath her. The man's breath caught in a smothered exclamation, then he strode across the deck to where an axe lay. He tore up a hatchway and seized a rope that lay nearby, then caught Gail and began lashing her to the improvised raft.

The next few seconds were ever afterward confused in her mind. The rope, the raft, the smothered choke of the water. Then she looked up frantically to see her companion dive from the rail into the sea as the dying ship gave a sudden lurch and groan and disappeared from view.

Tyndale House books by
Grace Livingston Hill
Check with your area bookstore
for these best-sellers.

Grace Livingston Hill

OUT OF THE STORM

LIVING BOOKS®
Tyndale House Publishers, Inc.
Wheaton, Illinois

This Tyndale House book
by Grace Livingston Hill
contains the complete text
of the original hard-cover edition.
NOT ONE WORD
HAS BEEN OMITTED.

Printing History
J. B. Lippincott edition published 1929
Tyndale House edition/1990

Library of Congress Catalog Card Number 89-50796
ISBN 0-8423-4778-X
Copyright ©1929 by J. B. Lippincott Company
Cover artwork copyright ©1989 by Steven Stroud
All rights reserved
Printing in the United States of America

96 95 94 93 92 91 90
7   6   5   4   3   2

GAIL Desmond was fast asleep in her upper berth in the steamer when the impact came and nearly shook her out.

She clung to the railing and summoned her dazed senses. There was a sound of things rending beneath her, a wild confusion of cries following an instant of terrifying silence, and then all else was obliterated by appalling clamor immediately set up by the frenzied little creature who belonged in the lower berth, who had been flung like a wisp of cloth across the stateroom and was lying on the floor half paralyzed with fear.

Mrs. Adelia Patton was a woman of wealth and refinement whose sole business in life had been to please herself. That Mr. Patton had early recognized this fact and obligingly taken himself out of this life leaving behind a goodly fortune had in nowise hindered her in the pursuit of happiness. Gail Desmond had not been with her two hours as her newly hired companion before she recognized the fact that her employer was the most selfish woman she had ever known. Clinging now to the edge of her crazily tilted berth, in this desperate situation, she had hard work not to despise the silly little woman who was screaming and wringing her hands and calling upon God to protect her as if she were the first concern in the universe.

With one quick dash of her hand the girl rubbed the sleep from her eyes and sprang to the slanting floor of the stateroom, kneeling beside the frantic woman and placing a cool steady hand upon her forehead.

"Mrs. Patton, be quiet, please. It won't do any good to scream that way. Are you hurt anywhere? Well, then please keep still till I can find out what is the matter. It may be nothing at all, and then, of course, you don't want to make yourself ridiculous. If there is anything the matter we shall need all our senses to get dressed and take care of ourselves."

Her calm voice arrested the woman's attention for an instant, but at the suggestion of anything being the matter she set up a hysterical scream that shivered through the girl's sensitive frame till she felt as if she could strike the woman. However, there could be nothing gained by two people's losing their heads, so she turned from her and hurriedly put on some clothes. Meantime, her employer lay huddled on the floor complaining loudly:

"You're an unfeeling girl to stand there taking care of yourself when I am dying of fright. Why don't you do something? We may be going to the bottom. We shall drown! Oh dear-r-r-r! we shall dr-r-rown! And no one cares for me. No one cares for poor little me. I might have known that a hired companion would never think of me when a time of danger came! No one cares for me!"

Gail turned and swiftly caught the little creature in her arms, set her upon her feet and gave her a shake.

"Be still!" she said indignantly. "No one could possibly care for you when you are acting like that. Sit down on the edge of the berth and put on your clothes quickly. We may not have any time to waste!"

"Oh, I can't! I can't!" wailed the poor woman, sinking down upon the floor again. "Don't you see I'm all unnerved, you cruel girl! You'll have to dress me yourself. What else am I paying you for? I shall certainly discharge you the minute we get to land. Such actions!"

"Mrs. Patton, look here," said Gail trying to speak calmly again, all the while fastening her own garments with rapid hands. "There isn't time for you to act like a child. It may be as much as our lives are worth to stay here. You must put something on while I go out to see what is the matter."

"Oh, you are not going to leave me here like a rat in a trap to drown, are you?" and the woman uttered another piercing scream.

At that Gail went to the door of the stateroom and threw it open regardless of the woman's protests.

A steward was hurrying by.

"Collision!" he said succinctly before the girl had time to ask. "All on deck at once!" And he was gone.

The girl's lips set firmly and she turned to her companion who had heard the word and was silent and wide-eyed with horror.

"Put this on!" she said sternly, seizing a large silk negligee, which was the only available garment at hand to cover the woman.

"Oh, but I can't go out on deck in that!" objected the vain woman. "Get that tweed suit of mine, that will be most suitable. And my hair, you'll have to fix my hair. I couldn't go out in crimping pins."

"There isn't time to get anything else," said Gail severely, "and the steamer isn't going to wait for sinking until you have dressed for the occasion. There is no time to arrange hair either."

She slipped the robe about her and fastened it quickly, fairly having to hold her still, for the woman had no mind to be attired so carelessly.

She was like a child, who when she saw the inevitable, succumbed and went wildly to some new extreme.

"You are a most cruel girl," she sobbed hysterically.

"Get my pearls at once. I must make sure of them. And my rings, where are they?"

Gail tossed the jewel case to the woman, more to keep her quiet than anything else while she hastily hunted out a long warm cloak and put it around Mrs. Patton's shoulders.

"Here is your purse!" She put it in the trembling little good-for-nothing hand. "Now we must go up instantly!"

"But my hair!" Mrs. Patton's hand went to her crimping pins. "And my face is all cold cream! I can't go this way!"

"Wipe your face on this handkerchief!" Gail thrust a handkerchief into her hand and pushed her toward the door. "Hurry!"

But the woman held back, her face blanched with fear, dreading what she might see on deck.

The strong young girl finally had to pick up the little, petted woman and carry her up on deck, staggering under the trailing robes and hindered by the frantic attempts of her charge to get away from her.

Once on deck Mrs. Patton forgot her bristling crimping pins and her besmeared face, and took to her life-long occupation of getting the very best that was to be had for herself.

On deck all was confusion, nobody paid the slightest attention to her. No matter what she had worn no one would have noticed. For the first time in her life she forgot appearances and began to look out for self-preservation.

Gail dropped her into a vacant steamer chair that had slid as far as it could when the deck slanted and then been stopped by a pile of life-preservers that had been thrown down in a heap. But Mrs. Patton did not remain idly on a steamer chair. She was up and away in her bedroom slippers with the agility of a bird, and when Gail turned back from looking this way and that to reconnoiter, her companion had disappeared. In dismay she looked about for her and caught sight of her flying down the deck toward a group of people where a boat had been lowered over the side. She saw her break wildly through the crowd into their midst, and when she pursued her she reached the place just in time to see her scrambling up on the deck rail. "Oh, Mrs. Patton!" she cried, but there was a look of cunning in the little, old eyes, the kind of look a miser has when his gold is endangered. Her life was her gold and she hoarded it carefully. Before Gail could reach her, or before anyone else noticed what she was doing, the woman was over the side, falling wildly into the midst of the already overcrowded boat.

For a woman as frail and dependent as she had been she righted herself from the fall with extraordinary agility, and perched like a magpie in the lap of a great gouty gentleman. She looked triumphantly up at her late companion and called out musically in her most dulcet tone wherewith she was wont to beguile those whom she has just bulldozed: "Miss Desmond! Miss Desmond! You'll have to come in the next boat. There really isn't room for any more here to be comfortable!"

The words floated up to Gail amid a chorus of profanity from sailors and others in the overcrowded boat, but Mrs. Patton sat serenely in her cream and crimping pins like a war chief in his paint and feathers, and ignored it.

"I wish you'd try to save my gray satin slippers if you get a chance," she called back in the same tone she would have used if she were starting out on an automobile ride. Then a great wave lifted the little boat, and the childish creature clasped her hands over her eyes and let forth another of her terrible screams.

Gail watched her for a breathless second, and then turned back, half feeling a responsibility for the foolish little gray slippers upon her. But a sailor pushed her roughly.

"Boat over there just starting, miss," he called as he rolled away. "Better hustle! ain't got no time to lose. This here boat's due to sink in about a minute more."

Gail flew up the slippery inclined deck, catching at the railing as she went, going in the direction the sailor had pointed. Some one tossed her a life-preserver and shouted to

her to put it on, and she tried to adjust it as she went, thinking as she did so of the stories she had read of life-preservers
and the people who stuck them full of pins so that they were
useless when the time of need came. Her father had used
something like that to illustrate unpreparedness for death, in
one of his sermons in those long-ago, dear days when he and
her mother were living in the quiet little parsonage, and she
was going to college. Blessed father and mother, gone two
years from earth, yet missed as sorely as at first. They were
at least spared the horror of this. They would not be on earth
to read the papers tomorrow morning and know that the
boat on which their beloved daughter sailed had gone down
some miles off the coast. They would not be there to watch
anxiously for news of her, to weep if she were lost, or wait
for days and weeks and maybe months and still be wrenched
by hope and fear.

Preparedness! She was prepared to go if it was God's will.
Life had been none too easy a place for her since her home
had been broken up. She would have few to leave now, and
had she not often felt the longing of a lonely Christian for
home and heaven and the satisfaction of being face to face
with Christ? To her, death meant no more dark horror than
the mere physical passing. She had long ago set her house in
order and felt that dying would be going home to God. Still,
there was the natural instinct of youth for self-preservation.
All these thoughts flashed through her mind as she hurried
up the deck struggling into that life-preserver, and wondering why she was not tremendously frightened. Her main
emotion seemed to be one of disgust for the selfish little
creature who had attended so thoroughly to her own affairs.
It seemed to her she would rather drown than make such a
miserable spectable of her own littleness.

She was not actually thinking, but merely being aware as with
a lightning glance, of certain facts. Her mind was really busy
wondering what she ought to do. The gray slippers, as they
should, had dropped away with a clear vision of the danger.

The deck seemed to be strangely alone all at once, where a moment before had been clamor and confusion. Only one man was standing where the group toward which she was hurrying had stood. He seemed to be hesitating, shaking his head and waving toward the boat below as if telling them to go and leave him; but at the last moment, just as she reached his side he evidently was persuaded. He was climbing over the rail as she came up.

As he saw her he stopped with an exclamation of horror that she was left behind, and springing back shouted below, "Wait, here's a woman!"

Already there was noise and confusion. "Too late!" she heard someone call, and "Look! The ship! She's sinking!" And even while they spoke she felt a sensation as if the earth was about to sink beneath her.

The first feeling of panic seized her then, but she shut her lips and gave mute appeal to the man with her eyes.

He was a big man, with strong well-cut features, and responsible eyes. His attire of sleeveless undershirt and trousers was too indiscriminate to place him socially, and when a ship is sinking beneath one's feet one does not stop to appraise one's only visible companion.

"What ought I to do?" She asked it calmly though her heart was beating wildly. It had come to her that this was the last minute before something dreadful was going to happen.

"Get in that boat down there, quick!"

He turned and motioned down below, but as they turned they both saw at once that the sailors were pulling out from below and were making frantic efforts to get away from the vicinity of the sinking ship. A green churning spot in their wake suggested a hidden monster sucking them down to horrid depths.

The man's breath caught in a smothered exclamation.

"Wait!" he said and strode across the deck to where an axe lay. With quick, strong strokes he tore up a hatchway and seizing a coil of rope that lay at hand caught the girl and began lashing her to the improvised raft.

"Oh, what are you going to do!" she murmured, but her words were like gasps. She began to think she knew what dying was like. And yet she took time to be glad she was not alone. It would have been awful to go down alone with a sinking ship.

The next few seconds were ever afterward confused in her mind. The rope, the raft, the smothered choke of the water, the realization that she was out away from the ship and was yet alive. Frantically she put out her arms to grasp at something, but there was nothing but the slippery raft and the rope that bound her. If the rope would give way she would be washed into the sea like an insect, so wildly the flimsy foundation under her was tossed to and fro.

It was several seconds before she remembered her companion. Where was he? What would become of him?

Then she saw him dive from the rail into the sea as the dying ship gave a sudden lurch and groan and disappeared from view.

2

GAIL thought the man had gone with the ship, for something appeared to strike his head as he went down and then
the water closed over him. Her crazy raft tilted the other
way, and a wall of angry green foam rose threateningly
above her head till she could see nothing else. The sinking
ship or the monster that controlled it kept sucking, sucking,
and the waves above kept towering, till it seemed as if they
were contending between them which should rend her or
submerge her, the waves or the depths. It seemed a long
time before the commotion of the sea subsided, and when
she could look again she thought she saw the man's head
floating with drifting spars and deck chairs and bobbing life-
preservers. One of these she caught as it floated close to her.
It seemed good just to get hold of something, to touch it and
feel there was something else besides herself and that raft.
She was becoming overwhelmed with her loneliness in the
sea. She strained her eyes, and tried to twist her body as her
raft turned, to see if the man were anywhere near. Then all
at once his body seemed to be hurled at her from a mountain
of green water, his dark hair floating like short seaweed. His

eyes were closed. She could not make out if he were conscious.

As she had reached frantically for the life-preserver, so now she reached out again and caught him by the hair and held him. So weak she seemed against that mighty force of water that was dragging him away from her. Yet it flashed upon her that she must hold him, must save him in spite of waves and death! He had given up his chance in the boat to save her. She owed him a life. If life were still in him she must save him. He had been struck. He could not save himself.

The thought seemed to lend force to her grasp, to infuse her with new strength. She sat up as far as her rope would allow her and grasped with the other hand, pulling him nearer until his head was on the ledge of the raft. Then she pulled at the neck of the light undershirt, but it was thin and tore. She must get hold of his shoulders. She must somehow lift him on to the raft with her. If it were not strong enough for two, at least she would share it with him while it lasted. They would go down together.

She pulled harder, and then she rested. One arm was lying across her lap now. It seemed lifeless and slippery and cold. The great knotted muscles that must belong to an athlete were like so much inanimate iron. How could she hold him? Yet she must.

The second life-preserver which she had caught! Could she get it around him? Wouldn't that make it easier to lift him? She had tied it by the strings about the rope, and now, holding her silent companion with one arm about his head and shoulders, she reached backward with the other hand to unknot the string. Her face was tense and strained. Her breath came hard, her position was unbearable. The blinding spray dashed wildly in her face at intervals, and the knots seemed welded of steel so soaked they were with salt water. Her fingers were cold and trembled. They stumbled and were clumsy. Her sodden nails turned back from her soft fingers, yet she stubbornly persisted, and at last succeeded in untying the knot, cautiously holding the ends with her fingers, lest the jealous sea should snatch her precious prey.

Somehow she managed to tie that cork jacket about the lifeless man, pulling the knots with her teeth and easing her aching arms by clasping them round his slippery shoulders.

When the knots were tied securely she dropped back and closed her eyes to rest. She realized that a greater effort yet must be hers if she would save the man. She held him as easily as she could to give her muscles rest, then struggled up and began once more to pull and turn and try to lift him on to the raft. At last a great wave lifted him, and would have washed him quite away beyond her reach but that she put forth all her strength and drew him to her, until he lay across her feet, his head thrown back where she could touch his face, one arm across her lap where she could hold him quite easily by a light grasp. Yet he had not moved nor seemed to know. Perhaps after all he was dead.

If only she could loosen the rope that he had bound around her, but he had drawn the knots tightly, and the water had swollen them. She could not get them loose. They would not move any more than if they were carved of wood. But she must fasten him somehow as soon as possible. Her arms were so numb, and her fingers so weak that any moment a vagrant wave might dash him from her, and she could not bear that so long as there was a spark of hope that he might be alive.

She tried to think if there was anything she wore that she could use to fasten him, but of the few garments that she had thrown on so hastily none were suitable for such a use.

She felt in the packet of her big streamer cloak that she had snatched as she hurried from stateroom. Joy! There was her long scarf that she had used to throw around her head while on deck. It was of silk, long and wide and strong, though soft and pliable enough to be folded into the ample pocket of the cloak. Quickly she snatched it out, and looped it around his waist, no easy task in her strained position, tying it firmly to the rope that lashed her to the raft.

Then leaning over she slipped her hand over his heart and held her breath. It was beating faintly. She could surely feel the soft thuds, or was that the beating of the waves beneath her?

She had to lie back again and rest, for the exertion had been very great, and she felt giddy. Her tired eyelids drooped a moment, then she opened her eyes wide and looked about. The big waves towered above her on every side. Did it take as much water as that to make those curving blue ripples that one watched from the boardwalk at a summer resort? How mighty was creation!

She turned hungrily to the inanimate form by her side. If he would only wake and keep her company in the awful wideness of the sea! She leaned toward him again. If only she could know he was alive! She knew so little about death. What was that test she had heard of once? Oh, a mirror held before the lips! The sea had no mirror. But she bent her face till her cheek was near his nostrils. Was it fancy only or did she feel a slight breath? Ah, how could she tell when the waves rose and fell with wide tossing and loud roar, now and again washing over their raft and wetting them completely?

She shivered even with her heavy clothing. The wind seemed to search through her and her flesh was like ice. What must it be for the man in his thin clothing if he were yet alive?

With infinite pains she tugged at her cloak until she had drawn one side of it out from under the confining ropes. Then she pulled it over her companion and crept as close to him as she could. It seemed warmer and less frightful so. She had a dazed feeling that her senses were slipping from her. She had never fainted in her life, but she thought it might be so that oblivion came. She sank back exhausted. The next wave that towered and broke and washed over them seemed to wash her life away, and blissful oblivion came upon her.

When she awoke again it was night and the stars were shining in a heaven infinitely farther away than the sky she had known all her life. The waves about her seemed to have caught some fallen stars and to be toying with them, tossing them back and forth from one to another as a miser plays with ill-gotten gold. Both the stars and their reflection were cold and indifferent like haughty things that did not see distress.

Strange fancies filled her brain at first. The water still on every side was the first fact that crept into her waking consciousness, and next that she was yet alive. Gradually she roused her stiffened body and reached out a hand to touch her companion. He was still there, and the arm next to her seemed warm, at least it was warmer than she felt. A great hope sprang up within her. Perhaps he really lived, for until now it had not crossed her thought how terrible it would be to be lashed to a raft on the open sea with a dead man!

If he lived what was there that she could do to help him back to consciousness? Nothing, unless she might help to shelter him from the terrible wind which had arisen during the night. She shivered and drew his head into her arms. It seemed as though there was warmth there. She almost thought she felt his lips move as she passed her hand over his face in the starlight. A frenzy of desire to bring him back into life again seized her. She drew him closer and tried like a mother to shelter him close. She even laid her own cold check against his and was surprised to find that where his face had been sheltered it was warmer than her own.

If he lived how long could he hold out against the blast, and the cold and the hunger?

She looked up to the sky to see if she could judge how far the night was on its way and found to her horror that the stars had been blotted out in that brief few minutes. Some drops fell on her upturned face. A new trouble faced them. A storm was on its way!

As if he were a child she drew her silent companion closer

into her arms, tenderly drawing the cloak over his arms, sitting up painfully that she might hold him closer. A fierce spirit of protection entered her. This man had given his life to try to save her. What little fragment of that life still remained was hers to protect while he could not protect himself.

Suddenly a light flashed out across the water! A long, keen, wide ray, that searched and quivered and was gone. It seemed to go over the heads from tip to tip of two waves, and they were hid in the hollow of its shadow underneath. She crouched and clutched the cloak closer round her charge.

The light flashed again, after what seemed an age of time, and then again; and after a time she began to understand that it must be one of those revolving lighthouses on the coast. She had watched them often from a sheltered pavilion where she had sat with her father when they were off together on a vacation. How strange that now such a light was her only connection with the world! She had never thought when she watched it idly in her pleasure that she would be in need of it afar on the black water. Would any watchers see the little speck that was their raft tossed like an egg-shell on the deep, and know that two souls, living or dead, were tossing there?

The waves roared on and the rain fell faster, and when she looked again the lighthouse seemed farther away. They had drifted past it, for the light was off to her right now, and it seemed to be much fainter.

So she sat and nursed her silent charge, and after awhile she fell asleep again for a time, with her head leaning against his, her sheltering arms still about him.

The morning was pale and gray in the sky when she awoke again, and there was a sense of warmth in her arms. When she lifted her head and looked at the face of the man, she thought she saw a slight movement of the lips and nostrils as if he breathed, but when she gently stirred him he made no sign, except that his head fell lower down upon her arm and settled softly there as if it were more comfortable.

She drew the cloak over his shoulder again and looked about her. The sky was heavy with clouds, and rain had settled into a slanting sullen drizzle. But off on the horizon when the raft was lifted on the top of a wave she saw a dark line. Could it be that this was the coast? Could it be they might drift near enough to be seen?

Anxiously she watched, and then turned to her companion. She was sure now that once or twice his lips moved, but no sound was audible above the pounding of the waves.

As it grew lighter she could see his face, and something in the expression brought back the capable, responsible, refined look he had given her when first he saw her.

With widening anxious eyes she watched the horizon, and now she was very sure that dark line meant the land, and they were drifting toward it. And then she sat and prayed, prayed as she had never prayed before, that they might somehow get to land and that her companion might open his eyes and live.

Out of the infinite it seemed to grow into a gray form of outline irregular at first with every league of onward drifting, until at last she could see houses, one, two, three, a dozen of them at least, separating themselves one by one from the gloom. There came the tense half-hour when the frail raft pounded and pitched and wavered and quivered, and hesitated on the edge of the entrance to a little quiet harbor, a sort of sand-bar where two ways, or seven, met and clashed in mighty fury.

How she prayed now with wide eyes fixed upon the land, watching every turn of the little craft, holding her breath when at last they took the mighty plunge across and floated to the right instead of to the left, plunging with the surf, and beaten and bruised, but all the while going toward the land.

Could they live through it? Could the man more dead than alive weather this last awful tumult of the sea reluctant to surrender its prey? "If God be for us, who can be against us?" she murmured aloud, and prayed the more.

And so by the hardest and the roughest, with the life and hope almost gone from the woman's soul, and the man still silent in her arms, they floated at last to the edge of the shore, and grated harshly upon the sand.

For the first time the girl looked about her, shivering at the furtive waves that laid a cunning head of spray upon her shoulder, as if even yet they might snatch her back to the deep. It was evident that the danger was not all over. The tide might yet turn and carry them back across that tumult into the wide sea again. They must get free. While they were still close to land they must get off that raft upon the shore and get beyond the clutch of the monster of the deep.

She laid the man gently down upon the raft and set to work upon the knots once more, but her fingers were stiff and sore, and her whole body was an agony of aches and pain. She looked wildly about, her heart still praying, and wondered what to do.

Then a possibility occurred to her. Would the man have a knife in his pocket? Could she reach far enough to find out?

She struggled into position again, and finally succeeded in getting her hand into his pocket. Yes, there was something there. A round, hard, smooth object. That would be his watch, some little trinkets, some money perhaps—and a long thing, ah, yes a knife! Her finger tips could barely touch it, but by and by she managed to get it in her hand and draw it forth.

It was a tedious task to cut that heavy sodden rope, but at last it was accomplished and she unwound the lashing and was free.

Then stepping out into the water, with all her might she pushed the raft up to the sand and dragged the man upon the beach. Panting and staggering under the load, she managed at last to get him on the sand where the water could not touch him, and then, almost ready to drop with weariness and faintness she stood up and looked around her for any possible means of help.

3

AT first sight the row of houses that were scattered along the beach seemed to be deserted. Was it an abondoned resort to which they had drifted? A strange desolation came upon her. Then she reflected that it could not be worse than the wild sea from which she had just come, and new courage filled her. She took a new survey of the place.

There was a great hotel of decayed splendor and massive wooden proportions, paintless now and weather-stained, with crazy shutters nailed to the windows, by rude cleats; that was at the extreme end. The place looked as if it had not been occupied for a decade. It was like a skeleton staring with its sightless sockets upon the scene where it once lived. The row of cottages following the line of a shackly boardwalk and a tumbled-down pavilion or two, varied in size and general dilapidation, growing better farther on. She looked carefully at each one in turn, but saw no signs of life until she turned and saw in the other direction not two rods away, a single cottage out almost upon the beach, the sand about its feet showing that the waves often approached quite near. One could fancy the spray dashing over the porch at high tide. The girl shuddered as she recalled her intimate association with ocean spray the previous night.

This cottage alone of all the dozen seemed to be open, the curtains blowing wide in the breeze, and even as she looked some one came out on the piazza, shook a rug and retreated within.

With a lingering glance back at her charge the girl started for this cottage.

The colored woman who opened the door was a neat elderly person in an indigo cotton gown and a white turban. She rolled the whites of her eyes, and let her loose under lip drop open in amazement when she saw the girl standing there in her soaked garments, with drenched hair hanging like a mane of dark ropes down her back.

"Great day in de mawnin'!" she ejaculated as she held the door wide open and stared. "Whar you done cum fum?"

"From the sea," answered the girl as quietly as if she had said "From the city."

"Land sake! Never did see folks go in bavin' in gyarments like dem. What you all want?"

"I've not been in bathing. It was an accident on the steamer. We've been shipwrecked. We've been out all night and just drifted in here. There's a man down on the beach that I'm afraid is dying. I want somebody that knows to come down and help me get him somewhere, and somebody else to go for a doctor, quick."

A pair of querulous eyes appeared behind the colored woman's shoulder.

"What's the matter, Corinne? I thought everybody was gone but us," said a shaky old tone.

"So dey is, Mis' Battin, so dey is. Dis yer gal say she done cum up fum de sea. She say dey got naxydunt and done ben shipwreck."

Corinne's hands were on her ample hips, her elbows bristling excitedly. Corinne had not had anything so interesting happen since the bowling-alley of the old hotel burned down. She was disposed to make the most of it.

"Won't you please send somebody down to help me right away?" said Gail, raising her voice clearly so the woman behind could hear. "I think that man may be alive yet, if there is somebody who knows what to do. Come quick or he may die."

"What is it? What is it she says, Corinne?" said the old lady, hobbling nearer on crutches. "Is she a beggar? We can't be bothered with beggars here. How in the world did she ever get here through the storm? You told me the grocery-boy had to come in a boat from the mainland, and you said even the telephone-wires were down."

"Yes, mom, I done say so," announced Corinne, settling back on her hips and extending her under lip argumentatively as she bobbed her head emphatically. "I done told you dem telefome wihes was down, an' I done tell you dat grocery-boy hed to sail ober in a boat fum mainland. I ain't tell no lie. I done tell de trufe."

In despair Gail flew up the steps and went to the old woman's side speaking close to her ear, clearly and distinctly:

"I've been shipwrecked and there's a man dying down on the beach. Please give me some help quick!"

The old woman drew back startled and looked at the girl with her little piercing eyes as if to make sure she was not insane.

"Shipwrecked! Dying!" she ejaculated, and then her hands shook and her querulous tone returned.

"Well, we're all alone here. I don't know what we can do. The people have all gone home. The last one left yesterday when the storm began. My son won't be back for two weeks, and the man that was staying with us to look after things got a telegram and he had to go home. We can't do anything," she whimpered unhappily, anxiously. "I don't know what we can do. You'll have to go somewhere else."

"But you said there wasn't anybody else here, and we can't go anywhere else. We haven't any way to go, and there isn't any time. That man has got to be taken care of immediately or there is not a chance for him to live."

"Well, what do you want me to do?" The old lady was almost crying. She was very excitable.

"Haven't you any blankets?" asked Gail. "Give me a couple of blankets quick, and some stimulant of some kind, and a hot water bag full of hot water. Quick! If that man dies it will be your fault. I've kept him alive all night. I'm sure we can save him. I think he's alive!" She caught her breath in a sob. "Won't you please come down and see if you can tell? I don't know much about sickness. You surely will know whether he is living. And please get me some blankets quick!"

"Get her some blankets, Corinne! In the downstairs bed room there's a pile. Child, I couldn't go down there. I haven't been down those steps without help for years. You mustn't ask it. I'm an invalid myself. I—I have to be taken care of myself. I—I—I—don't ever go out only to go home in the fall."

The old lady's voice was still complaining as if somehow the appearance of these shipwrecked folks was a personal injury to herself.

"Great day in de mawnin'!" ejaculated Corinne again, hustling off through an open door. "Brankets! What do she want ob brankets?" But she brought them, and in despair Gail seized them and started down the steps.

"Get me some stimulant or some milk or something quick, and something hot! We're both frozen!" she called as she ran. "Get something and come quick!"

She had almost reached the man on the beach when she stumbled in the long grass on the dunes and fell, bruising her hands on the sand-spurs and almost knocking out of her the little breath she had. She lay for a second gasping with fatigue, and prayed aloud as if God were standing close beside her: "O God, please send some one quick to help! I can't hold out much longer." Then she struggled to her feet and got to her knees beside the man.

The two women stood spellbound in the doorway, watching her as if it were some kind of a show they were attending, gesticulating, ejaculating; but when she fell and rose again to kneel beside that still, dark something on the beach, the senses seemed suddenly to come back to both of them, and they grew excited and alert.

"I b'leeve dat is a man, shor' nuf!" said Corinne lifting up both hands in horror. "It shor' is a man! My soul, it's a ma-an! Mis' Battin, what I do? W-w-what you done want I should do?"

The old lady's eyes were fixed on the kneeling girl on the sand, but her mind was keen enough now.

"Go get my aromatic spirits of ammonia, Corinne, first. It's on my little sewing-stand by the window over there. Yes, that's it. Now you go stir up the fire and put on some kettles of water to heat, and you fill the hot-water bag, and put on a saucepan of milk to heat. There isn't anything like hot milk to bring folks around."

Corinne hustled heavily off and the old lady, with a wild look around as if she thought the powers of the earth and sky might somehow object, hobbled close to the steps and began a slow descent. She could go down steps when she had a mind to, and this was one of the times she had decided to go.

It was raining a fine mist in a driving slant, and the old lady pulled up her little plaid shawl over her head and shoulders and defiantly plodded out into the sand. She was halfway over to where the man lay before Corinne returned and discovered her and hustled after her.

"Oh now, Mis' Battin, child, what you done do? You come right back in de house. What Mr. Sam going to say to me when he come back—lettin' you go way 'lone out in de rain?" But the old lady was determined now to go and ordered her servant most energetically.

"You go right back, Corinne, and bring those things!" she said standing still and stamping her foot in the damp sand. "Go!" And the black woman turned and fled.

"Oh, my soul!" she said, "Mis' Battin done got one ob her fits, an' what kin I do? Mr. Sam mos' kill me when he done git back foh lettin' her rampage around in de rain!" But she got the things and returned in a hurry.

By the time she came back the old lady was down on her rheumatic knees in the wet sand with her hand on the breast of the man, and holding the ammonia-bottle to his nostrils. A long shuddering gasp was the response to this, and the heart of the girl leaped with joy. By this time he seemed like her own child.

"You can't do anything with him out here in the wet!" complained the old lady, her sudden spurt of courage forsaking her and fear and sudden childishness returning upon her.

"Take me back to the house, Corinne, I'm all wet!" she cried, and the tears began to course down her cheeks.

As if she had been a petted child the woman lifted her to her feet and almost carried her over the sand back to the steps.

"Thar, now, honey, Mis' Battin, yoh poh little thing. Thar, now honey, don't you cry. I'se goin' to put you to bed and make a hot drink foh you, honey, so you won't get col' an' be sick. Thar now, honey, Mis' Battin."

The changing mood of the hysterical old lady took another turn.

"No, Corinne, nothing of the sort," she said sharply. "You'll go right up to the attic and get that folding cot that's up there by the stairs, and you can take it down there and help that girl get the man on the cot and bring him up here. I'll stay by the fire and drink some hot milk, and I'll be all right till you get back. Hurry now, quick!"

There was that tone again that Corinne had to obey. She set her mistress reluctantly down in the doorway and hurried upstairs after the cot.

"Great day in de mawnin'!" she muttered, " 'Zif I was hyahed to tote round grea' big dead men wid der shoes on.

Why don't he git up hisse'f an' come up here, I'd like to know. I don't like to be round dead men, anyhow, and Mis' Battin better look out, she git dis yer house hanted, an' den whar she be at? She can't git Corinne stay in no hanted house, not eber!"

Corinne lumbered up the two flights of stairs and thumped the cot down, step by step, talking to herself all the way.

Somehow they got him on the cot, and the two, the big fat servant and the exhausted girl, lifted it and carried him across the intervening sand to the house, staggered up the steps with their heavy burden, and into the bedroom off the sitting-room where the old lady stood waving a crutch like a brigadier-general and directing their slow progress.

Then suddenly, before the cot was fairly set upon its legs beside the comfortable-looking bed the girl crumpled in a heap on the floor. She had gone to the limit of her strength.

"My soul!" ejaculated the black woman, dropping her end of the cot and flying around to the girl. "My soul! She's done gib clean out! Now ain't dat a pity!"

The old lady was on hand with her aromatic ammonia and in a moment more the girl opened her eyes. She turned at once to the cot.

"We must get him warm and dry," she said as she tried to get up.

"No, honey chile, you jes' leab him to me," said Corinne in a caressing voice. "You leab him to me, chile; I'll put him in bed in no time. You jes' lie still a minute, and I get him fixed, an' den we'll ten' to you too. Pears like I'se jes got my ole brack hands full dis mawnin'. Mis' Battin, you sit down, please; you know you can't stan' up like dat 'dout gettin' lame. Now, Mister gemmen, we'll jes' git you out de way."

She stooped over capably, like one accustomed to care for the helpless, and began to pull off his sodden shoes and few wet garments, rolling him in a blanket and putting the hot-water bag to his feet. Then she turned back the covers of the bed, and hurried off to the kitchen, returning presently with several bottles of hot water wrapped in towels. These she laid in the bed, then stooped once more and lifted the great man, half carrying him, half rolling him, and put him into the bed, packing the hot bottles about him and covering him up carefully.

The girl had closed her eyes again and the old lady had thrown a big flowered comfortable over her. But she shivered in her wet garments and felt suddenly too weak and sick to lift her head.

"Now, honey, chile, you gotta git dem wet cloes off ur you boun' to cotch your deaf o' cole. Mis' Battin, what we gwine put on dis chile?"

"Eh?" said the deaf old lady, lifting a trembling hand to her ear.

Corinne lifted her voice mightily:

"What we gwine put on dis chile, Mis' Battin, some o' your cloes ur some o' mine?"

The old lady looked at her uncertainly, with a startled comprehension, "H'm! Why—something—anything!"

There was a sudden working about her mouth and the tears filled her faded old eyes. She turned away abruptly to hide her emotion. The old servant stood arms akimbo watching her, mingled pity and satisfaction in her face. Finally the old lady turned back.

"Help me up-stairs, Corinne. I'll go up and find something of Jeannette's that she can wear."

Corinne's face shone.

"Dat's right, Mis' Battin, honey. Reckon Miss J'nette won't need none o' dem follies up dar in de heab'nly kingdom, with all dem robes of righteousness, an' gold'n slippahs, an' dimon' crowns she's wearin' now. An' you all know, Mis' Battin, honey, dat Mistah Sam done tole you you oughta gib dem tings to some one what needed 'em. Dis chile needs 'em, sure nuf!"

She chattered like a magpie all the way up-stairs, and then

she came down thumpily, rolling her huge body from side to side as she set each ample foot upon a stair.

She took the girl up-stairs to the bathroom and helped her undress, turning on the hot water to take the chill off the room. She even helped her rinse the salt water from her long tangled hair, and rubbed it dry in a big Turkish towel. Then she got her into the nice clean garments that the old lady grudgingly handed out from a room that nowadays was always kept shut and locked. There was a soft warm bathrobe and slippers in the outfit, and when Gail was arrayed in these and her hair brushed out on a big towel over her shoulders to dry she began to feel more like herself, though her limbs were shaky and stiff from the long confinement in a cramped position, and her whole body felt weary even unto death. If it had not been for the responsibility of her fellow traveler she would have dropped down on the floor where she was and gone to sleep, feeling that she did not care what heppened any more. But more and more as she went through her hasty toilet she felt the burden of this life that she had taken upon herself.

Now that she knew beyond a doubt that he was still living she felt the responsibility doubly. If he should die now she would feel it had in some way been her fault. Perhaps that was not reasonable, but she felt it. He seemed somehow to belong to her out of the whole world to care for. By and by she might be able to find out who he was and send for his friends, but just now he was hers and hers alone, for God has sent him straight to her hand in his dire neccessity, and she had brought him so far safe.

A doctor! She must have a doctor at once. How could one be reached? They had said the storm had cut off communication with the mainland and there was no one to send. Well, then she would have to take a boat and go. She knew how to row. She would find out how far it was to the mainland and row there if there was nothing else to be done. Perhaps her strength was far gone, but she knew her will and nerve would hold out to get her there and send a doctor back, and then what did it matter? There was no one anywhere that cared very much what became of her—no one for whom she cared deeply now any more. She might as well die helping a man who had given his chance of life to help others. It was all in a lifetime anyway and what did it matter?

She was thinking these thoughts as she slowly descended the stairs with Corinne. But she was left to walk across the floor by herself, and the floor suddenly seemed to rise and enfold her to itself.

4

IT was some minutes before Gail came to consciousness again and she looked around her bewildered.

"I'm sorry to make so much trouble," she said, "but perhaps if you could give me something to eat I would be able to do something. I have a little money. I can pay you for whatever expense and trouble we are to you."

She spoke into the old lady's ear as she bent over her, and her hostess answered her sharply:

"Nonsense, child! Don't talk about pay!" For the thought had come to her, "What if this had been Jeannette?"

Corinne waddled up with a bowl of hot soup she had been concocting, and Gail ate it eagerly.

"I must get a doctor right away," she said as she ate, while the two stood watching her. "Could you tell me how to get there? Did you say you had to go by boat? Could I get a boat here on the island? I know how to row."

"Great day in de mawnin'! Honey! You row? You couldn't neber row to mainland wid yo' poo' little weak streng', and yoh poo' little white cole han's in all dis mis' an' stawn! 'Sides, der ain't no need. I done sent foh de doctah a'ready. De boy was here wid de fish fom up at de point an'

I tole him to go right quick, dat a man was dyin', an' he'd be hanted foh eberlast'n' ef he didn't git dat doctah here right-quick-away. So you jes' res' yoh bones, honey child, an' don' you worry none. Say, honey chile, is dat man you all's husband?"

"Oh, no!" said Gail with her white cheeks growing pink. "Oh, no, indeed! I don't even know him at all."

"He ain't no kin 'tall to you all? Den how you cum to brang 'im hyar?"

"Indeed, I never saw him before until I came out on deck and tried to find a boat," said Gail. "This man was helping people into the last boat that was left, and he was going to help me, but before he could get me over the rail the boat went off and left us and the ship began to sink. Then he tore up a hatchway and lashed me to it with a rope and just got me away from the steamer in time before it sank. I saw him spring overboard after me, but something struck him on the head as he fell, and after that I didn't see him any more till he floated by the raft, I caught him and held him, and by and by got him pulled up beside me. But he must have been hurt, for he never opened his eyes nor moved."

"How d'yoh know he wa'n't daid?"

"I was afraid he might be," said Gail, wearily closing her eyes, "but I couldn't take the chance. I held him on the raft till I got my scarf around him, and that helped to hold him. It was a terrible night!" She shuddered at the memory.

"An' you stayed on dat air raf' all night in dat big stawm wif dat air might-be-a-daid man! Wasn't you scairt?"

"I don't know," sighed Gail. These seemed such trivial questions.

"Yoh do' know! Yoh do' know! Mis' Battin, she say she do' know ef she's scairt sittin' all night on a ship-do' tied on wid a might-be-daid man! My soul, honey, I'd a jumped right out into dat sea an' drownded, I'd a been so scairt. An' ain't you got no idee 'tall who dat man might be? Ain't you seed him 'foh on de ship? Wasn't he one ob de pass'ng's?"

"No, I hadn't seen him before that I remember. We had only been out a night, you know, and the lady I was with was afraid of being seasick and wanted to stay in her state-room, so we didn't go about on the ship that evening at all."

"What cummed dat lady? You reckon she got drownded?"

"She jumped overboard into a crowded boat. No, I think she was saved. She always looked out pretty well for herself, and made other people look out for her too."

"An' she done lef' you, my pretty? Lef' yoh all alone on dat big ship to shif' fer hose'f? Wal, honey child, yoh want know my 'pinion ob dat lady? Well, she ain't no lady 'tall, that's just me 'pinion ob huh.

"An' so yoh don' know dat man 'tall. Well, now, ain't dat strange! Yoh don' eben know what's his name?

"I reckum I best look in his pants pocket an' see 'f I c'n find out. It might cum in mighty handy to know what to call him ef he should come to, pretty soon."

Gail suddenly roused herself and went over by the bed to look at her patient. She laid her hand on his forehead. It was warm and a faint look of life was creeping into his white face. Now and then he moved his lips slightly, but the face was upturned almost in the same position as when he was placed in the bed—thrown back with the chin up, a strong, well-cut chin, and the long dark lashes lay unquivering on his cheeks; lean, well-modeled cheeks. Now that his hair was drying and loosed up about his brow he looked young, almost a boy. Gail's heart was stirred with a strange emotion as she looked at him, so strongly, finely built, so splendid in the lines of his face and head, and lying there so helpless yet not dead. What could it mean? Had the blow on his head taken away his senses forever, and if so would it not have been better that she had let the sea have him rather than that he should live and not come into possession of his faculties again? No, for his friends would rather have the precious clay, and know for a surety how he died. Somehow she must find his friends, whether he was to live or die.

She turned to Corinne, who had brought the wet clothing and was fumbling in the pockets.

"Reckum yoh bettah take dis junk," she murmured, plunging her hand in the damp pocket and hauling it out again full.

Gail sat down and held her hands for the things. A handkerchief, first, some loose change, some trinkets of gold, cuff-links, tie-clasp, a couple of scarfpins, a curious little old-fashioned locket with the picture of a beautiful girl in quaint costume as if she were siting for her portrait that somehow oddly gave Gail a feeling as she looked at it that he did not really belong to her any more, only until she found that other girl. That was all, besides a handsome gold watch with monogrammed initials, and an elaborate fob hanging from a wide rich ribbon on which was clasped a small jeweled fraternity pin bearing the same initials on the back.

Gail sat with them in her hands, studying the initials, and the picture in the locket, and wondering about it all, a strange, sad sinking in her heart which she could not explain. It was as if she held the fragments of a life and happiness in her hands, and hers was the hand that must put them together again if they were ever to go on; and she was helpless and knew not how to perform her task. In that moment her life-long habit of prayer came to her assistance. Her heart was lifted up in behalf of this stranger who was for a time in her keeping. Inexperienced girl though she was, God had led her thus far and he would show her now what to do.

She studied the initials while the black woman watched her, and then looked at the silent man on the bed. But the old lady hobbled away to a desk-drawer and brought back a little box.

"You'd better put the things in there and keep them for him. Those clothes need to be hung up by the stove to dry. If he should ever need them again—"

She stopped short, for at that minute the man on the bed spoke:

"Wait! There is a woman! Don't cast off yet! There is a woman on board!"

His voice was clear and commanding, and the silence that filled the room was startling. Even the deaf old lady heard, and sat down suddenly in her rocking-chair. The black woman drew quickly near to her, half in fear, half in protection.

"What yoh t'ink he gwine do, Mis' Battin, honey?" she asked in an awed whisper, but the old lady shook her head and the tears began to gather in her eyes.

To Gail the words were like an electric shock startling her into new life. It was the call of the man who had tried to save her, to her who had tried to save him. It was the strange mysterious bond that bound them, two utter strangers, to one another. Each owed a life to the other.

Somewhere the girl had read a book or a story, it wasn't very clear, just a vague remembrance, on the theme of how far one was bound to the person who had saved his life. But there was no question of any such thing in her heart when she heard that clear ringing command. She rose from her chair on the instant and went to his side. She was drawn to stand by him, to try in some way to let him know that he had saved her.

She stooped over and took the hand that lay tossing outside the coverlet, laying her other hand on his forehead, which she noticed was growing hot and dry. Standing so with his hand in hers she prayed silently that somehow she might make him know that he had saved her; that he might come back to life if possible. And then, he opened his eyes for an instant and looked into hers, a straight, keen look that seemed to be struggling with some perplexity. Somehow he found a solution in her eyes, for a dawning look of understanding and relief came into his and the lids dropped once more as if he had never opened them. Just that flash of recognition and then he was gone back into the land of oblivion where he had been since his plunge into the sea.

Was this the end? Was he going to die now? Had that been the return of the spirit to things material before it took its final departure from this life?

She put her hand anxiously over his heart but found it beating distinctly. She listened fearfully lest his breath should stop, but the rise and fall of his chest, and the quiver of his nostrils, were distinctly visible. Do people die so, after enduring such terrible things, and then just go out? Suppose this should be the end and they should never find out who or what he was, and she would have only that look, and that one splendid sentence of his to remember as hers! Well, she would be glad to have just that. Something in his eyes and voice told her he was a man she would be proud to call her friend. If he had others who had a better right to him, at least the past night and day were hers alone, and she might feel this much of him, this look and this last word of saving her were rightly her own and no other's. It came to her how exceedingly lonely her life had been in the past two years that she was content to take joy from a dead man's look; that it had the power to thrill her.

Perhaps something in her look touched the heart of the colored woman, for she began to bustle softly about, fussing with blankets and quilts, and presently she stooped over the girl, gently disengaged her hand from the man's she still held, and made her lie upon the cot, throwing a light afghan over her.

"Thar, now, yoh poo' li'l' honey chile! Thar, yoh jes' lay down yoh haid on dat nice sof' pillah and shet yoh eyes an' go to sleep. Mis' Battin and Corinne gwine tend to dat man, an' yoh needn't worry. Yoh jes' take a li'l' sleep an' bimby yoh git up an' tend him yohse'f. Thar now, li'l' honey-chile, don' yoh cyah. De sea can't swaller yoh up no moh, an' dat man gwine git well, so jes' go sleep."

Gail sank down into the soft pillow and let the tired eyelids fall, not even trying to prevent the weak tears that slipped beneath her lids and coursed down her cheeks. It was very still in the room. The old lady and the colored woman sat like statues watching their charges. The girl drifted into sleep almost at once.

When she awoke again it was night and a candle was flickering somewhere on a high shelf, casting weird figures over the unpapered white paste of the wall. Some Japanese fans grouped in geometrical patterns on the opposite wall seemed like gaudy butterflies resting from a mad frolic. A tall vase filled with milkweed gone to seed rested on a shelf beneath them. The girl looked at them vaguely. The colored woman stood beside the bed with a cup and teaspoon feeding something to the still sleeper. He did not seem to object. He swallowed it without waking, for the spoon clicked back into the cup several times as if for more, and once she heard a long sigh from the man on the bed. But her body was too utterly weary to sense more than this, and her mind seemed unable to waken and take hold of the terrible questions that had pressed upon it before she slept. She closed her eyes again and let sleep drift about her once more, nor tried to open them when the nurse came to her with cup and spoon and fed her something warm and comforting.

It was morning when she awoke the second time, how late she could not tell, but the sun was shining in a broad band on the floor from a window she could not see. A doctor stood beside the bed looking at the man. She knew he was a doctor by the leather case on the floor at his feet, and by his look of self-forgetfulness as he studied the patient. She was instantly wide awake and trembling, every sense on the alert, but she would not stir. She must lie still and listen. She must watch without his knowing and discover just what he thought about the man, whether he would get well or not. For instinctively she felt he would not tell her. He would think her unfit to bear it. He would consider her only another patient.

She lay quite still and watched between half-closed eyelids. But the grave face told little of what was passing behind it, and the low gruff voice spoke only in monosyllables, directing the colored woman or asking a question. The old woman hobbled slowly in on her crutches, looking more feeble in the bright light of the day than she had in the gloom of yesterday. She stood by the doctor and asked a few questions in a low, querulous tone, and the word "concussion" figured in his low-growled answer.

"Why, concussion of the brain! That's dangerous, isn't it, doctor? You don't think he'll die here, do you? I don't know what we'd do if he were to die here while my son is away."

The tears were trickling down among the wrinkles, and a helpless look was on her face. The doctor's voice was kind though gruff, as if she were a little child. He patted her on the shoulder and told her not to worry. The young man looked strong and vigorous and he might pull through. He couldn't tell for a day yet, but all they needed to do was keep him quiet and give him the medicine and a little hot milk now and then if he would take it. He would return tomorrow morning as soon as the tide turned and see how things were doing. Then he turned to look at the girl in the cot.

Gail's eyes were wide open now, and the gruff old man stooped over and laid a practised hand on her wrist.

"Well, how are you feeling, sister?" He greeted her quite as if she had just come from the train. "Had a rough passage, I hear. But your pulse is good and strong. I guess you'll be all right with rest. I'll just mix up a little medicine for you to take to ward off a cold. You have a splendid constitution, I should judge, to come through all that fright and exposure, and I guess you're a pretty nervy young woman. The young man made a fortunate choice of a traveling companion from all I can hear about you."

A smile trembled over Gail's lips and lit up her face into rare beauty, and the old lady and the colored woman who stood looking on exchanged glances of admiration. They had not had time to notice the girl's appearance before.

Then Gail rose up, a faint color coming into her cheeks, and asked eagerly, looking toward the bed:

"What is the matter with him, doctor? Will he get well, or is he going to die?"

The doctor looked at her keenly.

"What is he to you, child?"

She looked at him with steady eyes.

"He saved my life, and I must save his if it is a possible thing. Is there anything that could be done that you have not done already?"

"Yes." The keen eyes were looking her over. "Yes. I could have a specialist here from the city to see him. If anyone on earth could save him Doctor Laudenberg could. He is the only one I know anywhere in this region that could do more than I could do."

"If he were your"—Gail hesitated for a word—"son, would you send for the specialist?"

"I most certainly would."

"How much will it cost?"

"About two hundred dollars."

"Then will you please send for him at once," said the girl quietly. "I can pay for that."

"Hasn't he any friends or family? I understand you are only an acquaintance. Couldn't we telegraph to his friends?"

"If he has friends I do not know who they are, and we cannot wait to hunt up the ship's record and take a chance on who he is. He turned back from taking his place in the last boat because he saw that I was being left behind. He waited to lash me to a raft and lower me to the water before he left the sinking ship, and he was injured as he plunged into the water. You see I couldn't stop to hunt up any friends."

"Do you mean you don't know him at all?"

"Not at all. I never saw him before until just as the ship was sinking. I don't even know his name, you see, and so I'll have to do the best I can for him till some one else comes, or till he comes to himself. I wouldn't feel right if I didn't do everything that was possible."

"That's a great deal of money to put up for a stranger, young woman. There really is no obligation on you at all, you know. He may pull through without a specialist. We're only taking a chance, that's all."

"We'll take no chances," said Gail, her eyes bright, two red spots on her cheeks. "How soon can that specialist be here?"

"Probably on the two o'clock train if I hurry right across to telegraph."

"Then please go at once! Don't waste a minute's time. And if there is anything that will be needed that cannot be bought here, will you please buy it for me and I will pay you."

Gail had risen in her anxiety and clasped her hands together eagerly. The doctor looked at her admiringly for one brief second. Then he held out his hand:

"I'll go at once, and I'll get what is needed and bring it back, but I want to shake hands with you before I go. You're a girl in a thousand! In fact, I doubt if there are many more like you in the universe."

He strode away without waiting to see the tears come into her eyes, as she sank weakly back upon the cot again half dizzy from her sudden rising.

"Now, honey chile, yoh go lay down again!" cried Corinne, rushing to her with a cup of tea and a bit of toast she had been making.

"No," said Gail determinedly, "I'm all right now, and I'm going to get up and take care of him. The other doctor from the city will be here at two o'clock and then we shall know what to expect. You didn't suppose I was going to let two of us stay here for you to take care of, did you? I had to get a little sleep before I was worth anything, but now I'm perfectly myself and I am very strong and well. Nothing ever hurts me."

The old lady hobbled up presently with a protest, but Gail would get up and go over to the bed. Presently the old lady touched her on the shoulder and motioned to her to come over to the other side of the room.

"My dear!" Gail saw there were tears in her eyes. "My dear, you mustn't think because I was a little stupid at first that I grudge your being here. I'm glad we were on the island to help you when you landed. If we had gone as we planned last week you might both have died. My son would be so glad that we could be of service to any one in distress, and particularly to such a good girl as you seem to be. Now you mustn't worry a bit about staying here. In fact, I'm rather glad to have company, for it's very lonely being here alone. I wouldn't have planned to stay only there were two other families going to stay till the end of this month. They changed their minds and went home the day after my son left. He would be terribly distressed if he knew they had gone. He doesn't like me to stay here alone. I never have before. So you see I'm rather glad you came to keep me company.

"Now, my dear, if you feel able to be up you ought to have some suitable clothing. You'll want to look all right when that city doctor comes, of course. You go upstairs to the left-hand bedroom; Corinne'll show you the door, and you'll find some things. You just look around and find what you want, and if you need anything more ask Corinne for it. They belonged to our little girl, my son's daughter, Jeannette. She died a year ago, and I couldn't ever bear to give them away before, though my son has often begged me to. He thought it wasn't right. But now the Lord has sent you right here to the clothes without any of your own, and I'm perfectly willing you should have them. No, it won't make me feel bad to see you in them. I'll be glad. Jeannette would like it. She was that kind of a girl, always wanting everybody else to have things and have a good time. Her things are all in the closet and bureau-drawers just as she left them. She only went away for a day or two to visit last summer, but there was an accident and she never came back here. So I'd like you to go up there and act just as if that was your room, and put on what suits you best. No, don't say anything. It's all right. I'm not crying because I feel I don't want you to have them, it's because I—well—I can't help it. You make me think of Jeannette, you know. She was about your size. She was just nineteen. She had long pretty hair like yours."

Gail took the little weeping old lady in her arms and kissed her.

"You poor little dear," she said softly into her ear. "I love you, and I know just how you feel, for I've lost everybody in the world that belongs to me."

HALF an hour later Gail came downstairs dressed in a little dark-blue gown with narrow white frills on the waist, and her hair, which was thoroughly dry now and fluffed in its natural waves, put up in a simple girlish fashion that made her look very lovely.

"Bress my soul, honey chile, yoh do look mighty sweet an' purty. It suttenly do my old eyes good to look at yoh!" said Corinne standing arms akimbo as usual in the doorway to watch her come down the stairs. "Yoh suttenly hab purty eyes, an' hair. It do seem good to hab a young pusson round agin!"

It was a strange day and a strange new world into which Gail had stepped. From a quiet round of waiting on disagreeable, unreasonable, selfish people, where she had nothing to look forward to but monotony and self-effacement, she had become the one to think and act in a serious matter. She had come through a set of most unusual circumstances, into a situation that seemed to have no parallel in her knowledge, and she had no precedent from which to judge what might be right except the Golden Rule, and her own sense of loyalty to the one who had so easily cast aside his own chance of life when he saw that she needed it.

Again and again she turned her eyes to the bed to look on the face of the stranger who had not hesitated a second to pass the crucial test. She liked to study the fine strong lines of the face that seemed more and more boyish as she watched it, and to wonder if in everything else in his life he would bear the test as well.

There was not much to be done until the doctor returned. The girl watched the clock and gave the medicine on the minute, learned how to get a few drops of nourishment between the tight-closed teeth and rejoiced to see that they were swallowed. The quiet hours passed, broken only now and then by low moans from the bed; not complaining moans but sounds that seemed to be rent through great repression from the soul of the brave man. Gradually these moans grew more monotonous but each one seemed to go through the girl's heart and fill her with a vague dread. Was all their effort to end in failure and death?

The doctor had promised to look up the ship's list and bring it back with him if possible. She must be ready to think quickly and know what to do in case there was a name that fitted the initials on the watch. She must have telegrams already worded to send in case she was able to discover for whom to send. She looked at the pictured face in the locket and wondered if this sweet girl were one who had a right to know of his danger. She set her well-trained mind to work on those telegrams and worded them, for father, mother, friend, so that they would not hurt too much and yet would tell the truth. And through it all she forgot herself completely.

Once she wondered idly how it had fared with her erstwhile employer, and whether she had found gentle treatment in the little boatload of refugees where she had so selfishly thrust herself. If Gail had been free she doubtless would have tried to look her up. But now, with the responsibility of a human life upon her, she could not think of it. The woman who had so lightly cast her off without taking a moment's thought for her safety could have no claim upon her, and she would far rather go back to a stenographer's life than follow the childish, spoiled creature round the world, even though it meant a big salary with luxury and travel. In fact, she had known after the first half-hour of the voyage that her new position was going to be anything but delightful. If there had been any way of turning back to land and honorably providing otherwise for Mrs. Patton she would have rejoiced to do so, even with no prospect of a future position.

She had brought her little all in money with her, a matter of three hundred and fifty dollars in bills sewed carefully into her garments, because she had a feeling that she must have money with her to get home with if at any time her position with her new employer should become unbearable. It had been with no idea that this relation would so terminate that she had made such preparation and withdrawn her small savings from the bank before leaving home. She had made this provision for a possible need because she had once read of a girl who was traveling abroad as a companion who had been dismissed without warning at the whim of an erratic mistress, without pay, stranded among strangers, with no way even to secure a new position, and with no money with which to pay her passage home.

Gail sat by the window of the lonely seaside cottage and looked out across the waters. In the day's brightness the sea smiled in heavenly blue with no likeness to the awful deep that had almost engulfed her but a few short hours before. She was glad that she had her money with her. Glad because it enabled her to procure for this stranger the means of life and health if such were anywhere to be found for him. Not for an instant did she think of herself, and what it was going to mean for her to be in a new part of the country, with no recommendations and no opening to earn her living. So long as that money lasted it should be at his service who had so easily put his life at hers.

As the hour drew near for the great doctor to come Gail found herself sitting with closed eyes, her whole soul lifted up with petition for the life that lay in peril. Once when Corinne had taken the older lady up-stairs to lie down, and her heavy feet could be heard trotting solidly overhead, she slipped from her chair to her knees by the bedside and laid her cheek against the hot hand that was tossed out over the white spread. It seemed as if so she might bring the suffering one closer to the attention of her God in whose power his life was balanced.

When the two doctors arrived they brought with them an assistant and a nurse. Gail caught her breath as she looked up with steady eyes and faced them. She thought she knew what that must mean, the possibility of an operation. For a moment her heart faltered over the long strain of anxiety. It did not occur to her that the patient was a stranger. Had he not become very near because they two had been shut away from the whole world with the deep while death stalked beside them for a time? Her heart tightened with the big responsibility she had taken upon herself.

The doctor handed her a newspaper which gave a brief account of the wreck at sea, and mentioned the names of a few of the passengers, but it did not give a full list of them. It spoke of a few who had been picked up by a passing steamer, and among the number Gail noticed first the name of Mrs. Adelia Patton, who had been taken at once to apartments in a hotel in New York. Strange that two days ago she and that woman were starting out for a winter's pleasuring, at least Mrs. Patton expected pleasuring, and she herself was a necessary part of the machinery to the end. And now here she was miles away from New York in a strange house taking care of a strange man about whom she knew nothing and Mrs. Patton presumably happy and not knowing but that she was drowned.

Well, she had no regrets for her lost position. Probably she could still have it if she telegraphed at once, or went after it; that is, provided the woman did not hold a feeling of resentment toward her for the severe language which she had used toward her in those last desperate minutes. But no power could drag her away from her present self-chosen responsibility and she felt sure that Mrs. Patton could find many more companions who would do her work as well as she could have done, and be glad to have the opportunity.

Things moved very quietly in the sick room after the specialist took charge. As if by magic they all assumed white linen uniforms, and all sorts of appliances seemed to be forthcoming from the suitcases which they had brought.

Corinne retired into other regions and began concocting a delicious supper, now and then slipping silently to the door of the bedroom and stealing away again, murmuring low to herself with a shaking head:

"Great day in de mawnin'! You tell me dat man ain't goin' die?" The old lady had retired to her room up-stairs, and the girl hovered in the background, quietly doing any little thing she could see was necessary, and keeping out of the way. She prayed for him within her heart. Since there was no one of his own near to pray for him, she would take that place.

It was an afternoon she would never forget as long as she lived. The smell of ether, the quiet workers, the low voices speaking only now and then like little signs to tell her what was going on, the grave faces, the silent man upon the bed. She was a very young girl with little experience, and she seemed to age during that time of waiting. She stood for a long time at the open hall door looking out toward the desolate sea. It had grown gray with storm again and was tossing and fretting itself into foam off against the sand-bar, as if some new victim were struggling hard against its power. Gail's eyes searched the vast gray greenness of turbulent water and wondered if even now some desperate mortal might be in torture and peril off there beyond her sight.

She realized at last how weary she was, and trembling,

dropped gratefully into a big steamer chair close at hand, closing her eyes. Why did she care so desperately about this man or boy or whatever he was whom she had helped to save from the sea? He was nothing to her. It was no foolishness of falling in love at first sight. Nothing of the kind. He had scarcely assumed a place and personality enough in her life for that. It was only as if she had seen some great splendid creature lying upon its back unable to protect itself against powers it might have conquered if it had not been for her. She must see that he had his chance. She must put him back where he was when he first saw her. Why, even now he might be lying comfortably asleep in a room in the Waldorf-Astoria, or some other chosen spot, if she had not appeared upon the scene and placed a duty between him and safety. It was she who had been the cause of his stricken condition, and she must put him back again if power of hers could do it.

Thus her thoughts went back and forth in a steady round, for what seemed endless hours. And then at last the doctor came and laid his hand upon her shoulder.

He had that exalted look tempered with awe that true doctors wear when it has been given to them to struggle with death and come forth conquerors, and his voice had a glad ring as he spoke:

"Well, child, we took the chance and found it was necessary. He couldn't have lived a day longer without the operation. If he lives now it will be due to you. We can't tell, of course, for a few days yet, what complication may arise, but so far everything is successful and he is doing well. Now, if I were you I would go to bed and rest."

Gail Desmond looked up quietly, trying to hold back the rush of happy tears that seemed breaking her throat and stinging her eyes, and smiled as she handed the doctor some bills she had been holding in her hand. They were neatly rolled together and still damp from the wet clothing from which she had taken them.

The doctor took it reluctantly.

"It doesn't seem right," he said, shaking his head. "This isn't all you have?"

Gail shook her head.

"Not all. I have a little more, enough for what I need. It's all right, please." The way she said it made him feel that he could say no more.

"Well, I'll give it to him," he said looking over to the specialist who was drawing on his gloves, "but I don't believe he'll keep it when he knows."

"Please do not tell him," said Gail. "It is right he should have his price. I have an idea the man would not care to be treated like a pauper. He does not look like that kind of a man."

"H'm! What about the way you're treating him? You say you don't even know him. Isn't that the same thing?"

"That's different," said the girl drawing herself up with pretty dignity. "We were fellow travelers, and I owe him my life. There is no such obligation upon either of you doctors."

"H'm!" growled the doctor huskily, "I was brought up to believe that we're all fellow travelers on this earth, no matter how we find each other."

He hurried off with the others to supper when Corinne called them.

6

THE nurse stayed three days. Then suddenly she was sent for to take another important case for the great specialist. She told Gail just what to do and the doctor said he guessed they could get along all right if Gail was willing to undertake the nursing. Gail said she was, and paid the nurse, rejoicing that she had not had to diminish the dwindling treasury any further for something she was quite sure she could do herself.

The patient was doing well, though there was a good deal of fever and all the talking he had as yet done had been to an unseen audience that peopled his own mind. Of the people around him who were doing for him he had as yet taken no cognizance. Not since that one long look he had given Gail on the first day of his arrival had he noticed any of them. Occasionally he uttered clear ringing sentences of decision showing that he was a person of strong opinions and character, but for the most part he talked incoherently in his sleep, moaning and tossing his head from side to side. He was kept under opiates most of the time.

On the third day, however, the fever began to subside and he slept more quietly. Then did the young girl take heart of hope and she watched every moment, scarcely taking time for the naps upon which the doctor insisted.

Sunday night he grew restless, and began tossing again. Once she noticed that when she spoke to Corinne he stopped his restless movements and seemed to listen. She sat thoughtfully watching him a few minutes, longing to try an experiment, yet almost afraid to venture without asking the doctor. When he began to move again and utter low sighing sounds she determined to try.

There was a worn Testament lying on Mrs. Battin's sewing-table, and Gail slipped out and got it.

Sitting down a little way from the bed by the open window that looked toward the ocean where the reflection of the pink and silver sunset sea was reflected on her sweet face, she opened the book to the fourteenth chapter of John and began to read softly, quietly, as one would read to soothe a child.

"Let not your heart be troubled: ye believe in God, believe also in me. In my Father's house are many mansions: if it were not so, I would have told you. I go to prepare a place for you. And if I go and prepare a place for you, I will come again, and receive you unto myself; that where I am, there ye may be also."

On through the beautiful age-old chapter of comfort and love she read, not daring to look up for a long time, not changing her position, nor raising her voice above a sweet low tone. Till she came to the words: "Whatsoever ye shall ask in my name that will I do, that the Father may be glorified in the Son. If ye ask anything in my name I will do it."

Mindful of her frequent prayers she lifted her eyes in one swift glance to the bed and back to the page again. She seemed hardly to lift her lashes, yet in that flash she found his eyes open upon her.

She dared not look again. She read on steadily, without a flicker of change in her voice, save now and then a tremble or a quaver as she tried to think what to do next. Should she read straight on until she was sure he was asleep? What had it meant for him to open his eyes and look at her like that? How she wanted to look again and make sure. Perhaps it was only a fantasy of her brain. Perhaps his eyes had not been open at all. Yet on she read, her heart struggling to keep its touch with the words, as if she knew she would lose her self-control if she did not keep her mind on what she was reading.

She was nearly to the end of the chapter. The pink and gold and purple light was flooding the room now, and there seemed to be a radiant silence all about her, as if the other occupant of the room had ceased his apartness and were keeping still to take part with her in worship. A sense of the nearness of God, of the Comforter about whom she was reading, filled her heart. Her frightened excitement quieted. She seemed to have taken hold of the words in the book and made them hers. She voiced the last verse clearly, tenderly with her own ringing trust in its truth:

"Peace I leave with you, my peace I give unto you: not as the world giveth, give I unto you. Let not your heart be troubled, neither let it be afraid."

Then, as if some power beyond herself were controlling her actions, she lifted her eyes in answer to something that drew her, and there were his open eyes still upon her in silent, intelligent interest! She felt at once that this was the real man in perfect control of his senses for the first time since his accident. At once her sense of protection was on the alert. She must be careful now what she did. She had been warned of this moment, and knew she might by some little hasty unconsidered word or action upset all that had been done. He would be very weak. He could not stand a strain of any kind. He must be soothed and made to sleep at once.

Without a sign upon her face of all that was passing in her mind she closed the book quite naturally and met his eyes with an understanding smile, as if they had been together in soul all these days while he walked alone in his darkness and had not known the world about him. She smiled and immediately the thin white face upon the pillow lighted with an answering smile and his eyes, large and bright with recent fever, hung upon hers wistfully as a little child might have done.

She smiled again, and nodded, rising softly with a quiet controlled movement so that his thought might not be disturbed, and keeping her eyes upon him moved close to the bed and took up the glass of medicine, stirring it gently with the spoon and putting it to his lips.

He swallowed the mixture obediently, his eyes still upon her face as if he feared it would vanish from him if he took his eyes away.

She smiled again, and stooped to lay the covers smooth about his shoulder. Then she settled down close beside the bed where he could see her quite easily without effort.

Because he seemed so wistful she laid her hand softly on his that was outside the spread. He looked down at the two hands strangely as though he undestood the comradeship in that touch; that she wanted to make him know she was here to help him through this hard place of weakness and silence. He smiled again when he looked up as though this little thing that she had done had made him more sure that she was real, not a figment of his imagination like all the others that had haunted him these days.

They sat so for some minutes, while the light on the sea died from gold and pink to purple, and the stars came out to set the sky for night. The shadows in the room grew deeper, but still she felt his eyes upon hers, and still she sat with tender smiling lips to help him understand his way back to life. Then slowly, reluctantly, as if he regretted his necessity, his eyelids drooped, and with a smile he dropped away to sleep, while Gail Desmond bowed in happy thanksgiving. She sat without moving for a long time after that, until Corinne came in with a light and tiptoed out again.

She slept but little that night, merely lying on the cot in a state of alert joy, ready to be on hand if he should stir. She kept the little alcohol lamp going under the chafing-dish to heat the broth she gave him at stated intervals. All through the night whenever she bent over him she fancied she saw still the lingering of that smile about his lips.

The doctor came early the next morning. The patient was still sleeping when he came, but while he stood looking down at him the man opened his eyes and looked from one to the other of them, lingering on the girl's face with that smile once more lighting up his own.

The doctor looked at her keenly.

"He is better!" he exclaimed. "Has he done that before?"

"Once. Last evening." Gail told him about it.

"H'm!" said the doctor, laying a finger on the patient's wrist. "Well, I can see the end of my job if this goes on. Well, old man, cheer up! We'll soon have you on your feet now!" he said to the silent man.

The patient looked at him curiously, pleasantly, but indifferently, then his eyes followed the girl as she moved to the little table and brought the clinical thermometer and the paper bearing the record of the past night. He watched her as if his very existence were dependent upon keeping her in view, as if his vision of her were the one thing that connected him with earth.

Gail, as she turned and caught that burning gaze felt her heart leap up with gladness, as a mother's heart leaps when her baby first recognizes her and singles her out from a roomful of people, honoring her with his smile. Her eyes met his and something seemed to spring from her soul to his, something of understanding and reassurance again, that gave him courage to keep breathing and looking.

"Don't let him talk," ordered the doctor just as he was going. "Keep him perfectly quiet and contented. Take your rest when he sleeps, don't let anything hinder that, and be ready to wake the minute he does, so that you can keep him from missing you. He's like a baby now, dependent upon his world, and you are the only thing in that world that he has recognized as yet. He'll cling to you and want you in sight all the time he is awake. You say you read to him last night? Try it again. What did you read?"

"Just a few verses from the Bible, something sweet and comforting."

"Well, that's all right, Don't try any exciting stuff. Keep the atmosphere calm and in a little you'll see him improving wonderfully. It's going to be a great strain on you now for a few days. He may be quite childish, but if you can hold out you'll be repaid in seeing your patient get well."

The doctor went away and Gail settled down to her day of nursing with a heart more elated than it had been for two years. There is something wonderful in having another soul dependent on you, in knowing that the sight of your smile opens life to a living being, and that you are missed if you even step over to the table out of range of vision. Gail fairly glowed with joy. Her face bloomed out in soft color, and her eyes shone like stars. She had always been a beautiful girl, but a sort of sadness had settled down over her features since the death of her parents that made her face seem a little cold and haughty. Now, however, she was fairly palpitated with life and gentleness and beauty. The old lady noticed it when she came down in the morning, and stood watching her with pleasure. Corinne noticed it and chuckled as she brought her mistress a soft-boiled egg and toast and coffee: "Bress my soul, Mis' Battin, honey chile, dat chile am so glad she's jes' like a summer mawnin' aftah a stawm. An' that sick-abed man's gittin' bettah. I done see him watchin' dat chile like he nebber laid eyes on a gal befoh! Great day in de mawnin', Mis' Battin, But I can't he'p thinkin' them two was jes' made fer one 'nudder, him a-gibin' up his place in dat ar boat, an' her a-grabbin' him and hangin' onto him through all that swashin' sea!"

It mattered no longer in that sick room whether the sun shone broadly over a smiling main of blue with little white harmless lacy fringes of foam that tossed up pearls on a silver beach; or whether the sea was gray and green and angry, swollen, livid copper with a leaden sky that threatened frightened scudding sails; or gray or gay, alike the sun shone in that room while those two woke, for always there were smiles and calm content and peace. The days went by with such sure, dear progression, such steady happy improvement, that the girl dreaded to look forward or back where this dear set-apartness was not, and where there would perhaps come a time when they might not be near each other, as now.

The first word he spoke—how it startled her—was in a whisper, "You are really here?"

She smiled and nodded yes, as if she understood how he had feared it was all his foolish fancies playing pranks, and he reached out a strangely clumsy thumb and forefinger and took the frill of her sleeve carefully between them in shy testing of her material reality.

She laid her warm hand upon his then and sat down beside the bed, and he seemed quite content to go to sleep in that way. More and more he would wake with a start, looking half fearfully about him, as if searching for her, and always met her look with a smile of illumination.

Every day he grew stronger now, and one morning wanted to talk, but she shook her head and laid her hand upon his and told him to wait until the doctor came. So he lay still and did as she told him. It seemed enough for him to rest and watch her, have her near, hear her voice. For now she often read to him, quiet psalms, and sweet comforting words of the Lord Jesus. Always he listened as if he enjoyed it. Once at evening when he had seemed restless she sang softly to him. His hand reached out to catch her sleeve as it lay along the arm of the chair near the bed, and he pulled her hand over until he could touch her fingers and press them feebly just to let her know how he liked the singing. After that when twilight came and the room was quiet he would utter one word:

"Sing!" and she would sing the songs she used to love

when she was a child, ballads, and hymns, and sweet fantastic things of brightness, simple and quiet and melodious. It semed as though he was blissfully content to lie and be sick if he could breathe forever this atmosphere of her presence.

There came a morning when he would keep quiet no longer; when he must talk, and know everything; when the springs of his being seemed to feel their strength once more, and his strong manhood would not be restrained. It began when he awoke. He caught her arm when she came to give him his breakfast, and announced that he was not going to keep quiet any longer. There were things that he must say, and he was perfectly able to say them and she must listen.

She laid a trembling hand upon his lips and quieted him, while she smilingly demanded that he eat his breakfast first and then she would see. But he was rebellious. He would not eat a mouthful even from her hands until she promised to answer his questions immediately after breakfast.

Though her heart was wildly beating, she kept him calm and promised he should talk by and by. She went on feeding him as usual, all the time talking about how fast he was getting well and how pleased the doctor would be when he came. She thought she had diverted him, and told him she had a beautiful poem to read to him when his breakfast was done, but he paid no heed to the poem, and when the last spoonful of gruel was swallowed he laid his hand on hers and said: "I thought you were going to leave me when I woke up. I want you to promise you will not go away."

"I won't go away as long as you need me," she smiled.

"Then you'll never go," he said and kept his hand on hers, looking into her eyes.

"Now, tell me, please. It was you, wasn't it, who came up just as the boat sank? I seem to have known it all along. I can't tell you just when I began to be conscious of it, but I've known it a long time. Now tell me, please, what happened? How did I come to be lying here like a boob and you wearing yourself out waiting on me?"

7

THE days of convalescence were slow and beautiful, the little group in the lone cottage on the Point each realizing that for a time they were set apart from the world to a special relation with one another, which was very delightful. Even their hostess felt this, and entered into her part with true spirit. She would come into the bedroom in the morning as if she had come to court to pay her respects to the king. And there was no humbler courtier than Corinne, who cooked delicious dishes and was never more pleased than when the young massa praised her newest concoctions.

In the dim watches of the night Gail duly warned her heart that this delightful companionship could not last forever, and that she must understand from the first that it was but temporary. Her way lay in the working world, and she could see from the start that the man had lived in a world of leisure and luxury. She cherished no romantic notions concerning what might happen in the future, but she resolutely set herself to be his friend and to nurse him back to life, with the sole intention of going out of his life when he was able to be on his feet once more. She had no delusions about the fact that this coming separation from him was going to be hard for her.

Never had Gail enjoyed such companionship with any man excepting her father, but this man was more than friend. He was child and rescuer and dear companion all in one. She knew that when she must turn away and go alone, the wrench would be extremely hard to bear. But because she had accepted this fact, and was steadily going on with her beautiful ministrations, their relation to each other was perhaps the more ideal. On her part, at least, there was absolutely no selfishness in it. As though they had been children of the same home, they went through the days, looking into each other's faces, frankly glad for the days that came each morning like new gifts, with the constant deference to one another that kills selfishness, and that utter joy in life that makes the soul blind to the fact that Edens do not last forever.

There was no love-making between them. The man basked in the sunshine of the girl's smile and loved to watch her every movement, but he made no claims upon her save those a patient or a dear child might make; the girl was utter devotion to him, anticipating every need and making pleasure out of his every whim. It was a little tarrying-time on the borders of life, where sin does not enter because of the nearness of Death whose castle lies not far away. That they must some day pass beyond that border and enter life once more and lose all this forever, each realized, but blissfully ignored. It was enough for the moment that things were as they were.

The September storms were over and a season of Indian summer had settled down upon sea and land. The long days succeeded one another with dreamy sweetness. The sea simmered and basked in the misty sunlight, as if a veil had been thrown over its terrors and only its liveliness shone through. The crickets chirped sleepily in the grasses on the dunes, and all nature seemed taking a siesta after the hard labor of the summer before it started in on the winter's arduous tasks.

In the cool evenings a fire burned on the hearth in the sitting-room, and its flickering light played through the open door over the bedroom floor. Mrs. Battin would sit before it crocheting or reading the paper, and they could see her from where they sat. She seldom came into the bedroom more than twice a day for a few minutes' formal visit, but the door stood open always and she was ready to help any suggestion of a need.

Mrs. Battin's son had not yet returned. His business kept him longer than he expected, and so he suggested that Corinne take his mother up to the city. But she preferred to remain at the shore as long as she had company, so the son was quite content, knowing that his mother was not alone. The elderly lady was becoming very fond of Gail, and she loved to watch her going about in some of Jeanette's pretty frocks, just as the other dear girl used to do. Gail also was growing fond of her. The querulous old tone had almost disappeared, and the look of discontent was giving place to quiet peace.

Sometimes she came and sat with folded hands while the girl read aloud from the Bible at evening, and then she slipped out again like a shadow when the reading was over. Gail's reading had become a daily ceremony, which even Corinne attended, slipping into the sitting-room and sitting just out of sight by the bedroom door, with her hands folded reverently in her apron. The old Bible was working its miracle charm that it always works whenever people give it an opportunity. The words were sinking into the hearts of the listeners and making them thoughtful. It is just possible that if the house had contained other books the Bible might not have had so good a chance, but the Battins were not great readers and the house was destitute even of magazines. It is to be supposed that the young granddaughter may have had books at the shore which probably had been sent back to the city home, and there had been no one about to bring more. An occasional newspaper was about all Mrs. Battin's eyes would allow her to read. So the Bible held full sway over this unique household, and the time set apart to it was looked forward to with eagerness. Gail entered into the reading of it eagerly, a new joy in the book coming to her own heart. And as she read new wonders opened to her sight.

Perhaps her rendering of the words had much to do with the interest of her audience. Her voice no longer chanted the words in a low monotone calculated only to soothe the soul to sleep. She read as if she were painting vivid pictures before her listeners' eyes, making every scene of the Bible live before them, bringing out unconsciously the thoughts from hidden passages until they had new meaning to people who heretofore had been but careless readers when they read at all. It is safe to say that to the young man at least the book was utterly new. To the others it suddenly became the word of God in very truth.

Gail, having been trained in Bible lore from babyhood by a father who was somewhat unusual in his spiritual life and his study of the Scriptures, unconsciously made clear, by her very way of reading, things that in the past always had seemed obscure to her audience. Without any knowledge of what she was doing Gail was becoming a preacher, and the sermons were all the more effective in that they were sinking deeper into her own heart as well. She had been so busy and sad and hard pressed in the two years since her father died that she had given little time to the study of her Bible, and so had grown into a more or less cold-hearted Christian. The daily reading was helping her back to a fuller realization of the presence of the Christ whose follower she had been since early childhood.

The young people did not talk about themselves. They almost went out of the way for a long time to avoid the subject. It seemed as if they feared to ask questions lest it break the perfect beauty of their present companionship.

When the young man asked for the story of the wreck Gail told it most briefly:

"You remember how you lashed me to a raft? Well, you

were struck on the head as you were jumping over the rail, and it made you unconscious for a time; but we floated to this harbor, and the doctor has fixed you up all right. He says you oughtn't to think about it now till you are quite strong. Don't you think we would better not recall it yet?"

He had nodded acquiescence, but he lay a long time looking at her and thinking. He remembered something. He wondered if it were true. He would have liked to ask her—but not yet. Some time he would if all went well. And then he looked at her and smiled with something in his eyes that she could not understand; something that made her heart leap up with unbidden joy.

"Isn't there some one to whom you ought to send word?" she asked him presently. "I should have asked you that at once. Some one must be very anxious about you all these days."

He looked thoughtfully at her again, a kind of a far-away, dreamy speculation in his eyes, then a half-comical smile grew about his lips.

"No, I guess not," he said slowly; "there is no one who would waste time fretting about me. Mother died when I was a kid; I can't remember my father. I've an uncle out in California, but I doubt if he even knows I was on that ship. The fellows might care, but I won't let them know yet. They'd think they had to trail down here and see me, a great mob of them, and I don't want them. Not yet. Things are all right as they are. They'll be glad to see me when I get back, but no damage will be done by waiting a little. But how about you? I'm afraid you have stayed away from your people to take care of me."

"I haven't any people," said Gail, trying to smile cheerfully, though her voice sounded pathetic. "Father and mother died within six months of each other a little over two years ago. I was the only child. There are no near relatives. A cousin by marriage on my father's side is the only one who even pretends to keep any track of me at all. She secured the position for me with Mrs. Patton, the woman with whom I was traveling South when the accident happened. She was very much relieved to get me off her hands, although I never have been a burden upon anything but her conscience. I fancy she would know nothing but relief if she heard that I was drowned. She might be a little sorry, perhaps, but it won't lose her any sleep."

"But how about this Mrs. Patton? Have you sent her word? Or was she lost?"

Gail entered into a merry account of her last scene with Mrs. Patton and he laughed heartily over her description, looking at her tenderly afterward and wondering if it were selfish in him to be glad she had no other ties to take her away from him.

Thus they drifted happily through the days of his recovery, learning more every day of each other.

The first day he sat up for a little while he asked for writing materials and said he must write some letters.

Their hostess provided all that was necessary, and the young man wrote three—one to his bank, one to his tailor, and another to a department store.

He slept a long time after that effort and awoke very happy. He declared he was going to get up as soon as his new clothes came.

Gail felt a strange sinking at her heart when he announced that. Not but that she wanted him to improve as fast as possible, but it made her feel that the time was short. She must soon go back to the lonely world and find something to do. This experience would be like a beautiful dream that was gone. She was like a person on the verge of waking before the dream is finished, lingering and trying to stay asleep. Yet she knew that the waking had to come.

The day his things arrived they had a happy time unpacking. Gail unwrapped the packages and would only allow her patient to sit up and direct. There were a large express package and a new trunk full of things. The express package contained a suit and overcoat. In the trunk were shoes, socks, undergarments, shirts, neckties, collars, and cuffs, a number of toilet articles, and a soft felt hat. Gail opened them and spread them out for him to see, handling the things with wistful fingers, glad that they were so soft and fine in quality, yet feeling by their fineness so much the more separated from their owner. She had known he would be like that— everything fine and fitting.

She helped him with his first toilet, brought hot water for his shaving, put in his shirt-studs and cuff-links, and fastened his tie. It all seemed so strange, but he was happy as a child while her heart was like lead. She could not keep back the tears or the lumps in her throat, and she had a strange sense of inward weeping, as if her heart were crying. Now and then she shook herself away from her melancholy and told herself how glad she was that her prayers were answered and that he was almost well, but when she saw him fully dressed, clean shaven, standing erect for the first time since his illness, the wall of separation seemed to rise between them and she could not help feeling shy. This was not the child she had sheltered and saved, prayed for and nursed, who was dependent upon her for his very existence. This was a full-grown man, with a tremendous will of his own and a keen delight in having come to his own again. She shrank back into herself as she would have done on shipboard if some accident of the day had made him her debtor for some trifling favor. Now she felt that this was a stranger with whom she must be reserved. He should see nothing in her to make him think she had laid any claim to his notice. She was just a passing stranger now whom fate had ordained should help him over a hard place and then pass on.

He was so elated with the idea of being dressed and feeling himself a man again that he did not notice her distant manner at first; but toward night, when he was tired and wanted to rest, when he needed her help she gravely gave it. She fed him his supper and patted the clothes about his shoulders, for the evening was chilly. Suddenly he reached both hands up and took her face between them gently, looking at her.

"You're tired," he said with conviction. "I've been a bear and a baby, and I've made you tired."

"Oh, no!" she said, trying to smile in the old way. Something in his eyes was speaking to her own and making it very hard for her to sit there that way with his hands upon her face, yet she could not shrink away and hurt him. He would not understand. They had come to a place where he would not, must not understand.

"Yes, you are tired," he said again. "You have been very good and dear to me. I haven't tried to tell you yet how I feel about it. I couldn't! I wasn't strong enough! But some day I'll show you!"

Then he let her go. She thought he had meant to show her how tenderly he felt toward her. It was a rendering to her deep gratitude and esteem of his heart. She understood and accepted it for that alone, and entertained no sentimental ideas concerning it. It was something sacred and sweet for her to remember always. Yet she lay long awake that night on her cot in the sitting-room, where she slept, with tears upon her cheeks, for the loneliness that was to be hers now in the near future. She tried to think what she should do and plan for her going, but could not. She must wait and let things take their course. She had trusted her life to God and she felt that she would be guided.

The next morning she slept late, and found to her surprise and dismay that her patient had dressed himself and was awaiting her in the big chair by the window. It made her feel as if her work were done and there was no longer need for her to stay.

He noticed her grave face and rallied her upon it, telling her she was going to be the patient pretty soon and he would have to play nurse, for she had been overworking. But she roused herself and tried to be gay, and the breakfast which

Corinne brought for them both on a big tray and put on a little table between them passed off very delightfully. Nevertheless, Gail had a continual feeling that she was a guest and ought not to remain.

Gradually, she grew accustomed to his being a man up and around. She still waited upon him continually, trying to save his strength which he would not save for himself, though he was growing stronger every day. He began to have a healthy color, and soon the doctor allowed him to take short walks upon the beach.

They would go out in the early morning, Gail carrying wraps and a rug and pillows, and walk a little way, then they would drop down upon the sand and stay a while, watching the sea, talking a little, resting, then walking on again, and back to their cushions for another siesta. Now and again Corinne would come out with a tray of something good to eat, or a glass of egg and milk for each. The still beautiful days of Indian summer slipped by to the dreamy chirp of the cricket, with that sad sweet pensive way that such days go in a lonely place where time seems to have stopped and necessity drives not mortals to forget the beauty of the autumn.

One curious thing about their companionship was that they had never as yet called each other by name. Neither could quite be satisfied to say mister or miss, and anything more than that seemed to break the unique relationship they had established, and so they drifted along with saying "You."

Gail had not even known his name until the day his letters came addressed in care of Mrs. Battin, to Mr. Clinton Benedict. It seemed a beautiful name and fitted her idea of him. Sometimes she longed intensely to ask him about himself and his life, but determined not to break through his reserve.

Their days of converse were very sweet. They talked about intangible things—souls and why they were made, tendencies and how far they could be controlled, character and what constitutes it. They settled all sorts of abstruse problems, and found out each others' opinions and preferences on a hundred thousand important and unimportant topics. They told stories, and dreamed dreams together, and almost Gail forgot her fears and shyness and blossomed out again into the frank, free-hearted friend she had been when she was nursing him; and always yet she was the nurse, alert for his comfort, husbanding his strength.

Then one bright morning they went forth as usual with pillows and shawls and the morning paper to find the most sheltered nook not far from the cottage. Gail arranged a place for her patient and settled him comfortably, and was just about to read the front page of the paper to him when the wind caught the sheet and shaking it open scattered its various leaves in confusion around her.

Laughingly she reached out hurried hands after it, and Benedict too caught a page as it floated by. As chance would have it the page he caught contained the society column, and was headed by the picture of a beautiful girl. With a startled exclamation he drew it to him and read a paragraph, his face a strange mixture of emotions; but when he looked up to meet Gail's questioning eyes joy had the predominance. She could see he was very happy and excited, and very much surprised about something. It must have some connection with the girl in picture.

8

"I must go to the city at once!" he said, and a weight like a mountain fell into the girl's heart. "Isn't there a morning train some time? I could get that fish boy to take me across and catch it. He's due to come in a few minutes now, isn't he? It is quarter to ten."

"He usually comes at ten," said Gail, trying not to show how much her voice was shaking, and how wildly her heart was beating. "But you are not fit to go on a journey yet."

"Oh yes, I am," he laughed; "I feel as if I could walk miles this morning. It won't be a hard trip. The boy will row me over and I'll take a cab to the station and promise to take a nap in the train. Besides, it's something very important and I really can't wait. I'll tell you all about it when I get back. There isn't time now."

He began to gather up the wraps and pillows as any man would, forgetting that he was still a patient and not allowed to carry anything.

She took them gently from him, her chin quivering as she struggled to keep back the tears. He looked down, and seeing her expression almost broke through a resolution he had made, but saved himself just in time.

"Don't look that way," he said, and his eyes searched hers so lovingly that she almost broke down. "Don't please! Trust me just a little while. I'll come back safe and sound. Why, I'll take you with me if you want me to. Then you'll see that I don't overdo."

But she laughed and shook her head.

"No, I can't go," she said decidedly; "but I wish you would wait till the doctor comes. I feel sure you are trying your strength too soon."

"No," he said decidedly, "I'm sure it will not hurt me; and I really must go. Look, there comes the fish boy! I must hurry! You needn't come back to the cottage; I'm all ready to go just as I am. Why don't you stay down here and rest a while?"

But she hurried along by his side, determined to see that he was safely started, choking back her tears and smiling like a summer sun between the clouds.

."It really isn't a funeral, you know," he smiled at her. "I'm coming back tomorrow night or the next morning at the latest. I may be back tonight, but I think that is doubtful, for I'm afraid I can't get at the people I want to see right away. But I'll try."

"Oh, you are going to stay all night! But you won't take care of yourself!"

"Yes, I will, I promise you. Now don't look that way. I'm coming back very soon, and I'll have something to tell you when I come."

Those were his last words again when they stood beside the little fish-boat that was to take him across to the mainland. He held her hand for just a moment and looked into her eyes with that wonderful deep look of trust and admiration that thrilled her to the depths of her soul. Then he pressed her fingers close in his, with a touch that was like a caress, and stepped in the boat.

She watched the little boat as long as she could see it across the bay, and when it was out of sight she turned and walked far away, alone, down the empty beach and let the blinding tears have their way, the choking sobs breaking forth from her sore heart. He was gone! She loved him, but she would not see him any more. That was her conviction.

By and by she controlled her tears. There were Corinne and Mrs. Battin with sharp eyes to see. She must not show how she felt. She went down by the edge of the sea and dipped her handkerchief in the water, bathing her face, salt to the salt tears to wipe them away. Then she walked slowly back to the place where they had left their things, and where a short hour before they had settled down for a pleasant morning. How suddenly it had come to an end! How sharp and quick had been the call! What had it been that stirred him so that he had found he had to go to the city at once?

She had dropped into the sand and thrown her head down on a cushion utterly weary of mind and soul and body, but now she remembered the newspaper. Which page had he been reading? What was it that had called him back to his own world again?

She reached out a trembling hand and drew the page to her. The picture caught her eye. A beautiful girl! "Miss Dorothy Taber Standord has announced her engagement to Mr. Arthur Hanson Briggs. Miss Stanford is the daughter of Mr. and Mrs. Ortley Stanford, of Dartwood Manor, and will be remembered as having led the opening march of the Carnival of Flowers, held last spring in this city, with Mr. Clinton Benedict, who was lost in the recent disaster of the Baltic."

Gail read no farther. She dropped the paper and stared off to sea, her eyes growing wide with understanding. He had then gone at once when he had heard that this girl was engaged to another man. He had said he would return and have something good to tell her. Of course it was easy to see what it all meant. He had likely been engaged, or as good as engaged, to this Dorothy Stanford, and the girl when she thought him dead had turned to another admirer. It did not speak well for the affection of the girl, but evidently the young man had been sure of her, and known that if he could only get to her she would turn back to him, for witness his delight when he looked up from reading the note in the paper. He was not distressed. He evidently knew that he could set everything right. Perhaps her people had wanted this second match all the time, and had pressed it upon her now that her former lover was supposed to be dead. There were a hundred ways to explain the thing, and her heart beat slowly in dull thuds as she thought it out, accepted it, said to herself, "I told you so! I warned you not to let yourself care!" Then she sat and faced an ocean that had suddenly grown gray and monotonous under a sky that had lost all of its sunshine.

He would come back and he would tell her that he was engaged to this beautiful girl. She looked at the pictured face in the paper. How could she bear it? He would want to introduce her perhaps, and have the girl thank her for all she had done for him. Terrible! She would never bear it! No, he might come back, but he would never find her there! He would never tell her! She had guessed it for herself, and she would fly away where he could not look in her eyes and see how she loved him. For she could never hide it now. She could not smile in the old dear understanding way, for this girl in the big transparent-brimmed hat would ever be between them. She had been a fool of course, but she would not stay to show it. She would hide herself somewhere and get work and work hard and forget it. For had she not known all along that she would have to forget? She must not spoil the perfectness of their friendship and of this season of intimate association which had seemed as holy and sacred as a friendship in heaven. She would go now, this afternoon, before he could possibly return. If he had had need of her still she would have remained no matter what it cost her, but now that she knew there was another girl to look out for him she was free to go and hide her bruised, foolish little heart in good sensible hard work.

She would have a hard time convincing the kind friends

in the cottage that this was necessary, for they had protested greatly about the going of Benedict, but it must be done. She got up hurriedly and gathered her cushions and went back to the house.

Corinne met her at the door.

"Now, yoh honey chile, yoh bettah go lay down. Yoh look peeked, yoh sho do. Yoh ben nussin' dat ar big man chile too long, an' yoh need res' honey. Yoh jes' set down an' eat dis yer nice li'l' bowl o' soup C'rin' ben makin' foh yoh, and den yoh go lay down."

Gail tried to eat the soup, but every mouthful seemed to stick in her throat. Nevertheless Corinne and Mrs. Battin hovered over her until she swallowed it all, and she managed to keep a smiling face until she got away supposedly to rest. It was going to be terribly hard to tell them, for they really seemed to care for her, and Mrs. Battin at least would miss her, she was sure. Nevertheless, she could not stay, and this was the best time to go; for the man who was hired to look after them had returned two or three days before, so they were perfectly safe and would not be alone.

Gail went about for a few minutes among the things that belonged to that other girl who was gone from all the perplexities, cares, and joys of earth, and was safe at home forever. She straightened up everything, put a few little necessaries together in a small bundle, and dressed herself in the simplest thing the borrowed wardrobe contained that was at all suitable for traveling. She counted out her remaining money, and found she had enough to pay a reasonable sum for their board, pay for her journey, and have just ten dollars left. That would be enough to keep her a week until she could find something to do. She surely could find something in a week.

She sat down at Jeannette's desk and wrote two notes, one to leave with the board money on the bureau where they would be sure to find it, the other to Benedict, to be given him when he came back.

When she had fixed everything she looked about for a second on the peaceful little room that had been such a haven to her in her necessity, and then she knelt for a moment beside the bed.

"Dear Christ, go with me and take care of me. Stay with him and take care of him, and keep him safely wherever he is. I thank thee for the blessings we both have had. Make me strong to bear the hard things."

Then she went out and down the stairs.

She had planned her going to be ready just when the grocery boy from the mainland would come over with the day's orders, so that she would have little time for discussion with the kind friends downstairs before it would be necessary for her to leave.

It was fully as hard as she had expected. She told Mrs. Battin that she had seen some advertisements in the morning paper, and felt she ought to go and look up something to do at once. She thought this would be a good time to go when her patient was away and would not need her.

The poor lady, of course, begged her to stay until next week, when they would all go up to the city together. She said Gail could stay with her for a while until she found the right place. But Gail smiled and protested and had her way. They told her that Benedict would be disappointed that she had gone during his absence, and begged her to be sure to return on the evening train so that she might be there if he came back that night.

She did not promise, but she did not hint that she would not be returning. She let them think what they would, only telling them not to worry, and thanking them for all they had done for her and her companion.

When she tore herself away from their protests and their loving advice at last, and hurried after the whistling grocery boy, they stood together, those two who had so stolidly received her on her arrival, and wept as they saw her disappear from their sight.

"Yoh reckum dat chile ain't runnin' 'way from him, Mis' Battin, honey?" asked Corinne, as she turned with streaming eyes to go into the house again. "Yoh reckum dey done hab it out an' 'greed to paht? Yoh reckum dat's why he went flyin' off so suddent dis yer mawnin'?"

But Mrs. Battin's kind old heart was too full for utterance.

"Bring me my shawl, Corinne, I'm all of a tremble," she said in her old querulous tone, and she went and sat down in Gail's rocking-chair and stayed a long time reading the Ninety-first Psalm, and trying to remember the girl's voice as she had read it.

Out on the bay the girl was straining her eyes to catch the last glimpse of the weather-beaten old cottage on the beach, while the grocery boy whistled a jolly tune.

9

GAIL Desmond, when she made her hasty escape from the haven by the sea and started out into the world again, had no intention of merely going to the near-by-city where she knew Benedict was bound. Her goal was New York, and once there she felt pretty sure there would be no danger of being found again. She did not rest easy until she was seated in the New York express with her ticket bought and a six hours' ride before her. Then she leaned back, and let her sad thoughts have their way. It did not matter now if her chin did tremble and her lips fail to keep back the sighs that came unbidden to them. No one would notice. She was sitting in the last seat in the car, with vacant seats all about her, and the train was rushing away from Washington as fast as it could go. Benedict, if he came back to the shore at all, would never know now how her heart was breaking. She had covered all her tracks and he would never find her.

Why was it that she had to meet such a man only to know that he was not for her? Why had a loving Providence seen fit to let her suffer so? But no, she would not question the Guiding Hand that had brought her through the sea, and let her save a life. She would be glad of that always, that she had been able to save his life who had been so willing to lose it for hers.

She did not see the hurrying landscape through the open window. Her eyes were closed and her thoughts were holding sad communion with herself. The jarring of the car beat the plush of the seat cushion into her wet cheek and made its impress there; the monotonous chant of the train put her to sleep. Perhaps her good angel stood over her sorrowfully, who knows, and pitied the poor lonesome child who was so rapidly rushing away from the little bit of heaven that had been hers for a few days.

About that time Corinne, back in the cottage by the sea, was standing over her mistress, making her drink a cup of tea and eat a bit of delicately browned toast, and saying speculatively:

"Mis' Battin, honey, yoh reckum dat chile done runned away from dat man 'cause she feel pride? Yoh reckum she 'fraid he tink he gotto take her 'cause she brung him safe tru dat ar stawm? Ain't nuttin' like pride to make a gal run away from a man like dat. Yoh reckum dat's de trubbel, Mis' Battin, honey?"

The hours passed on and the exhausted child in the back seat of the New York express slept soundly. The porter passed through and gave the last call for the dining-car, but she did not hear. For the time her troubles were forgotten. In her dreams she was sitting on the beach again at sundown, talking about the little sand-snipes pattering on the silver-pink sands with their little lavender kid feet, catching sand-crabs for their supper, and fluttering neatly back from each saucy wave that tried to wet them. There was a smile on her lips as she dreamed, and her sorrow fell away for a little while and let her sleep in peace.

It was evening when they reached Philadelphia and there was time to go out for something to eat, but Gail sat back apathetically. She did not feel hungry.

People began to crowd into the train. The seats filled up

and some were standing in the aisles. A family of foreigners with numerous cross babies came across the aisle and swarmed over into her seat. They smelled of garlic, and were sticky and sleepy, poor babies. Gail looked down at their little tumbled heads in pity and forgot for the moment her own sorrows in wondering what there was in life before their young untaught feet. Life all seemed such a puzzle. Would they find the way and follow the light up into the real day, learning to bear the tests as they came to them one by one? Was there any way she could help them? That was her creed, but how uninteresting it looked just now. She was standing a test. This necessity for her to flee from what she could not help counting dearer than her life was her test of course, yet it seemed more like a sharp stabbing pain sent to blind and stun her. Could she pass this test and come out bright and happy as God wanted her to be? Could she ever look on it as just one of the hard things of life that must be? Would it ever get over seeming like the end of all things for her?

It was late evening when they reached New York. She had never been there but once before, and that when she went with Mrs. Patton to sail on the voyage that had ended so tragically. She climbed the great stone staircases to the street and stood uncertainly at the entrance of the Pennsylvania Station looking out into the lighted world. Where should she go at that time of night to be safe? Should she hunt up the Traveler's Aid who advised lone women travelers, and ask to be directed to the Y.W.C.A. or should she just stay in the waiting-room for the rest of the night?

She decided on the latter course, for her ticket to New York had cost two dollars more that she had counted on, and she must be careful. Eight dollars was a small sum on which to face an unwelcoming New York alone. Of course there was still Mrs. Patton whom she might hunt up and claim for a mistress if she cared to do so. Mrs. Patton would at least be likely to give her a recommendation and let her stay with her until she could find another place, heartless little creature though she was. But all her soul cried out against appealing to Mrs. Patton, so she turned back and spent a weary night in the waiting-room, with only a sandwich and a glass of milk to eat.

In the morning, fortified by another sandwich and a cup of tea, she took her way confidently out into the great world to find her place. She had made herself as neat as her limitations allowed and did not feel troubled about her appearance. She had a theory that there was always plenty of work to be had if one was willing to do it, and she had little doubt but that she would find it without much trouble. She was met at the outset, however, by a difficulty that she had not anticipated. There were fees to be paid at employment agencies before anything could be done, and she had no money to spare for fees.

Wearily she walked the streets, going into pleasant-looking places and asking if there was a place for her. She bought a paper and studied the advertisements. Gail had been taking care of herself long enough to realize that there were dangers in the world. She had learned to preserve a quiet dignity among strangers that was a protection in itself. But her knowledge of any city life was limited to what she had gleaned from the books she had read and rare visits for a few days under her father's careful protection. Moreover she failed to estimate her youthful beauty at its true value and realize that even in her simple rather old-fashioned costume, she was a marked object wherever she went. It troubled her greatly to find that men were staring at her as she passed.

Toward evening she grew frightened at the thought of her dwindling treasury and went back to the station. There was a couch in the inner waiting-room and she could sleep anywhere, tired as she was. Surely by tomorrow she would find something to do. She thought of the Y.W.C.A. again, but did not like to spend the money for a room if she could help it until she was sure of some remunerative employment.

The couch was occupied when she returned to the station, but before midnight it was vacated and she was glad to stretch herself upon it and fall asleep immediately, too weary even to think of all her troubles. The shipwreck and Clinton Benedict by this time seemed to be only a myth of past ages, instead of something that had really happened to her. It seemed that she always had been tramping the streets of New York hunting for a job and that no one wanted her.

In her dreams the dear immediate past came back to her. She was again in the cottage by the sea, only now it was herself that was lying like a patient in the big bed with Clinton Benedict waiting upon her.

She started wide awake and found that there were tears upon her cheeks, and a large German woman, with a fat baby asleep at her breast, was watching her from the big rocking-chair near-by. The dull whir of a great city boomed on through the night outside, much like the booming of the sea.

The next day proved no better. A cold drizzle of rain had set in and the mist from the river and the mist from the ocean seemed to come in from both directions and envelop the city. Wherever she went people were cross, and kept her waiting a long time, often standing, so that she grew footsore and weary beyond expression, and her appearance became draggled and forlorn. She had to invest one of her few dollars in an umbrella, and the light serge coat which she wore was scarcely thick enough to keep her from shivering. The evil thought came to her that she had been a fool to give up her money for another who was doubtless fully able to pay his own bills.

Yet even in her extremity she was not sorry for what she had done. Perhaps she had not done wisely as some men count wisdom, but how could she have done otherwise? She had to get the specialist. The outcome had proved that Benedict would not have lived without the operation. And she could not go away without paying the doctor, and leaving something for their board and trouble. Doubtless Benedict would return and try to do something also. That was right, for she had left but a small pittance for such royal reception as had been given them all these days. Besides, there were the clothes she was wearing. They were not many, but they were worth far more than the money she had left. And so she dismissed the thought.

That night she went to the Y.W.C.A and took a room, but the next day and the next brought no more success in securing a position. Now there stalked beside her grim Want, with menace in his mien, and he waited for her outside every office she entered looking for work. It seemed incredible that with so many positions as there were every one was filled before she got there, or for some reason she would not do. Perhaps the draggled condition of her garments had somewhat to do with her losing some of them. At one place it was necessary that she speak and read Spanish, another wanted references, which of course she could not give without waiting to write to former employers; a third would take only an elderly woman; a fourth had decided to take a man, and so on. She tramped many weary miles, and used an incredible number of precious nickels taking long rides in the subways and elevated trains.

At last one night she was sure of getting a position to take care of three little children at the seashore. But she lost it because she didn't have caps and aprons to wear and the new mistress would not advance the money for them. She came back to her room utterly discouraged with just twenty-five cents between herself and absolute want.

Fifteen cents must go for supper. She had had nothing all day but a glass of milk and some crackers. She must eat now or give up and die. Tomorrow her next week's room rent was due, and she had nothing with which to pay it and so she must move out. There would be ten cents left to get breakfast. Five of it would buy a glass of milk and a tiny envelope of crackers, with the other five she could telephone to the

Waldorf-Astoria to Mrs. Patton. She had come to it at last! There was nothing else to be done.

Sitting sadly in a corner of the big dining-room with the clatter of dishes and conversation going on all about her she ate her fifteen cent supper and tried to be thankful for it, but hunger had gone beyond itself, and it seemed almost impossible to swallow anything. Perhaps she ought to have taken only a glass of milk again when she was so tired and weak, and saved the other ten cents. When she had forced down the last crumb, she went out to a telephone booth and called up the Waldorf-Astoria. She had meant to wait until morning, but she concluded that when one had a disagreeable thing to do it was just as well to get it over with at once, and there seemed to be no chance of anything better turning up by morning. She had exhausted her list of possibilities.

After much waiting she got the number and asked for Mrs. Adelia Patton. After another long delay and some explanations she was told that Mrs. Patton had left the day before for California and expected to be gone all winter. Yes, she had gone with a party of friends. Yes, she had a companion, a Miss Denworthy who used to be with her.

Gail hung up the receiver and sat back in the little booth faint with dismay. This was the last straw. What could she do? Her situation seemed hopeless.

After a time she mustered courage to creep up to her room and throw herself on the bed. She was too tired to weep. She just lay there and breathed, every breath a slow sob. It seemed to her that the end had come. This was no test. This was just plain being up against it. Had she done wrong? Ought she to have kept her money when another was in need and she the only one by to help? Ought she to have stayed down there till that young man came back, and let him pay her for the things she had done for him?

Her soul came to itself with this thought. No, never! A thousand times rather die of starvation than have that experience reduced to dollars and cents. No, she would compel herself to forget her misery and go to sleep now, and in the morning she would go out and force a living from the world. It was always darkest before the morning, and surely, she thought, life could be no darker for her than it was at this moment. The morning must dawn bright, she would make things come her way. Was it not her courage that Benedict had praised over and over again? She must have courage now.

So at last she fell asleep.

WHEN Clinton Benedict started on a sea voyage on the Baltic he had a definite purpose in mind. He wanted to get away by himself and think. Matters in his life had become so perplexing that he felt a crisis had arrived. He was not altogether sure of himself. He wanted to get away from everything that was distracting and find himself again and know where he stood.

When Dorothy Stanford first crossed his life he had thought her the most beautiful and accomplished young woman he had ever seen and had turned to her as directly and frankly as a flower turns to the sun.

She had smiled upon him with that subtle, dreamy smile of hers, looking at him tantalizingly from half-drooped lashes; gazing admiringly up into his face when they were alone as if he were all the world to her; averting her eyes with a long sweeping look and a turn of her head, or a coquetish appeal to some other man when in company. At first he had thought this charming, as if their friendship were a thing too sacred to flaunt before the world, and he had cherished her words and tones and glances as if they were jewels, every one more brilliant than the last. But of late her attitude had grown torturing. She was always slipping away with someone else, always having some beautiful excuse afterward, with that flowerlike droop of her slender neck and head, just where the light could catch the polish of her soft dusky hair that set her face off like a misty frame. He could but forgive her when she drooped her head like that, showing the tiny curl on her white neck where the hair was drawn upward. Dorothy Stanford had been canny enough to keep her own beautiful hair and a certain graceful manner not common among modern girls. She knew the charm of being unique. If she had copied other girls Benedict would not have looked twice at her. She knew this and was always careful to make much of her sweet old-fashioned pose when in his presence. It never occurred to him in those days that Miss Dorothy knew the value to a hair's breadth of that curl and attitude.

She certainly was a most popular girl in Washington, and her admirers flocked after her everywhere. It seemed selfish in a man to insist upon so young and beautiful a girl tying herself down to him. She told him sweetly that she did not think it was right for her to make so momentous a decision at once. She was young and just out, and it wasn't fair either to him or to herself. What could a man say to a thing like that? It seemed true. Yet he could not go away and leave her, for when he wavered from the deepest devotion and tried to forget her charming face she called him to her side with one of those adorable smiles and made him think she was the one and only woman in the world, and that in her secret heart she worshiped him.

There came a time when he could no longer rest on such a basis. He had insisted on some understanding between them, and she had reluctantly consented to an engagement, but declared it must be kept secret for a time, that she would not have her good times spoiled so soon, and when he tenderly reproached her and told her that if she really loved him her good times would be just the beginning, she pouted and called him cross. And then she would be so adorable with her shy upward glances and her thrilling smiles and caressing words that he would forgive her again.

It had been a trying summer. They had been at various seaside and mountain resorts, at house parties galore, and had seen much of one another, yet always at a distance or in a large company, and Dorothy had managed it so that she was far oftener seen with other men than with himself. Moreover there had been numerous occasions recently when she had not kept her promises to him, and had gone instead with someone else when he had been waiting for her. She always had a plausible excuse and looked so sweet in giving it that he would relent, and excuse her to himself, and sometimes even look tender over her childlike innocence in not knowing that she was hurting him. She seemed a little, gentle, tender thing to be protected and loved and forgiven always because she was of different clay from men, just a little soft thistledown butterfly thing that must not be troubled with thinking about big questions like love and honor. She was white and blameless of course. He could not think of sin or blame in connection with her.

One night she had tried him beyond endurance, looking into the eyes of a man whom he had warned her against. And finally she went off with this man during a time she had promised to himself. In his very face she did it while he stood with folded arms and sad reproachful eyes looking at her as sternly as he could bring himself to look at one he thought he loved. She had tried to smile it away and wave a good-bye to him, but when she saw his face there came a look of Eve turned out of Eden into her eyes, and thinking of it afterward there was no word that he could use to describe her but slinking. It seemed that she had slunk ashamed away from him.

At midnight when he walked in the lovely grounds of the mansion where they were staying, he came upon the two standing in the moonlight, the man's arm caressingly about her, her eyes looking up into his face.

Benedict had a gentle reasoning talk with her, and all her excuses were prettily made, with a tear here and a smile there, yet somehow the memory of that moonlight vision would not be dispelled, and her words seemed emptier than usual. Their relations had become more and more strained, she insisting that it was her right to do as she pleased at least until her year was up, and he was troubled and perplexed. Could it be that he did not love her after all?

It shocked him that her power over him was waning. He began to find himself questioning whether her excuses were always sincere. When he tried to look back and recall their conversations there seemed but little substance to them, and yet of so fine a fibre was the man that it hurt him that he harbored even for a second such thoughts of her he thought he loved.

Thrice he tried to get away from it all by deliberately refusing invitations where he knew she was to be, thinking thus to leave her free to go her way. But always she managed to call him to her side, so that he was not long away. Once he went after he had refused an invitation because she asked him to do it for her sake. He wondered why she wished it afterward. It could not be just that she might have more to give her admiration. He would not think that of her. And when she set herself to please him he would fling his doubts to the winds and trust her in the face of everything.

He grew grave when others were gay and she rallied him on his solemnity. He hunted out the grandmothers and the little children at the house parties and gave them a good time. In this sane atmosphere his moral perspective cleared and he was able to see things more rationally once more. Dorothy Stanford lost some of her glamour and appeared, in bald simplicity, a selfish, silly, pretty, empty-headed little flirt. Only his strong sense of loyalty still held him to her. He began to long to get away from it all somewhere, regretting that he had arranged to be absent from his business for the entire summer.

At last he took a decisive step. A short sea voyage seemed to offer him the quiet and leisure he desired. He left with very brief farewells the summer resort where Dorothy Stanford had taken up her court for a couple of weeks, and set sail.

During the quiet and the beauty of that first evening on shipboard he had sat apart from the throng of travelers, avoiding all acquaintances, and looking off to sea trying to get a comprehensive view of himself. He watched the heaving green-blue sea turn into purple with golden flecks. The horizon line of crimson and gold was rent with heavy thunder lines of blue and gray that betokened a storm. He saw the stars come out and the silver moon come up from somewhere behind the world and make a path of silver across the purple dark. He felt the infinite beauty about him. Before he went to his stateroom he had fully made up his mind to break with Dorothy Stanford, and to do it before his return to her world. He knew by many experiences that if he tried to break with her, face to face, she would find some way to hold him as she had done many times before. Now he was convinced she did not care for him, almost convinced that he did not care for her. For as he had sat looking off at the vast heaving sea in its panoramic beauty his soul had seemed to grow large and strong and something that had bound him seemed to break and set him free. Dorothy Stanford's arts and wiles dwindled away into trifling toys, and life looked full and fair before him. There were things to live for if woman had proved false, woman of course meaning one particular woman who, for the time being, represented all to his mind. When he went to sleep that night it was with no feeling of loss or longing for the trifling girl who had played with him so long. He had resolved to make his life big with other things, and leave woman out of consideration entirely.

When therefore, Gail Desmond in the wild panic of the

catastrophe dawned upon his startled mind and gave one look out of her clear eyes into his and asked in that cool quiet voice, "What shall I do?" he was startled even in that stressful moment to find that woman still had power over him. Of course he must help a woman. That it meant the risk of his own life was nothing. He had never been a self-centered man, nor a coward, and these days he was not holding his life very dear anyway. Maybe the biggest, broadest thing he could do with it was to lay it down to save even a woman. Women were more helpless than men. They could not help being what they were perhaps. They used their arts to get what they wanted because they had no other way of obtaining their desires. They were helpless and therefore a strong man must help them in a time of need.

That was his last conscious thought before things got too strenuous for him to do anything but act.

When he awoke after long dark smothering hours of mental distress, he found himself the weak and helpless one, lying in a strange bed. And a woman, an unknown helpless woman, was taking care of him and being eyes and ears and voice and hands and feet to him. He looked on her face and lived in the light of her eyes. Gradually he acquired the knowledge that this helpless woman with the wonderful true eyes and the pure face had saved his life. Somewhere back in those hours of stress and storm and wild waves he had a memory of soft arms and his head pillowed tenderly, but he could not be sure that it was anything but a hallucination. He used to lie and watch her in those slow days of convalescence when he seemed to be swinging on a hair between heaven and earth. It seemed to him that all that kept him from going out entirely was her smile. It seemed as though he had never known a real woman before, or perhaps this one was an angel. She grew into his soul from day to day as if she fitted there. Dorothy Stanford was as if she had never been. The very memory of her had dropped away.

When he came back into life again far enough to really

think and remember more than vague impressions, he thought of Dorothy Stanford. He was amazed at himself that he could ever have thought he cared for her when all the time there was in the world this wonderful, tender, beautiful dream woman who moved about him with a sort of occult sense of what he needed; whose spirit signaled his through smiles and the lighting of her eyes at every moment of the day or night when he was waking and needed her.

Later when moral sense and honor returned to guard the way he knew that just as soon as he was well he would find Dorothy Stanford and set himself free from any cobweb chains that bound him. He knew now beyond a suspicion of a doubt that he did not love her, and never had.

After all, his whole mind had been so taken up with Gail Desmond during those beautiful days of recovery, that Dorothy Stanford became a mere infinitesimal speck on the horizon of his happiness. A speck that must be forever wiped off some day if she did not disappear of herself, but so small a speck that she was seldom noticed. In fact if it had not been for the man's fine sense of honor there would have been no real reason to feel himself bound in the least by a girl who had so plainly violated all possible limits of honor in her treatment of him. And why? He was forced to admit now that it seemed to be because of her love for playing with men and subjecting them to her charms.

The very morning that the wind took a part in the story and flung the society column straight into Clinton Benedict's hands with Dorothy Stanford's face looking guilefully up to him, he had decided when he first woke up that that day should see a letter written to the girl which would make her understand plainly that from this time forth she was nothing to him. But when he read the heading of the column under her picture, "Dorothy Stanford Betrothed to Arthur Hanson Briggs," his heart leaped up with joy, for Dorothy had saved him the trouble of writing the letter. He read the paragraph about the announcement of the engagement with growing delight, laughing aloud as he took in the reference to himself as drowned. Then for a second his impulse would have made him turn to the girl beside him and tell her of his great love for her. But again the honor which held him to a fine straight course throughout his life put out a warning hand. Better go at once and see Dorothy Stanford and then he could come back to Gail with a clear record and tell her all.

It was the joy of that returning that fairly shouted in his voice when he bade Gail good-bye and told her he would have something to tell her when he returned. That joy that she thought was all for the girl in the newspaper.

All the way to Washington he was not thinking of what he would say to Dorothy Stanford; he was dreaming of Gail Desmond's eyes and the way she smiled when he was tired. He remembered her clear profile as it had looked against the sunset sky the night before, or the soft brown waves of her wonderful hair, shining as if touched with gold, or her voice at twilight as she read a Psalm, and his soul was thrilling with the love of her. It was because her presence seemed to be with him that the journey did not tell upon his new-found strength. He rested in the thought of her as he had rested while he was recovering.

When he reached Washington and took a cab to Dorothy's home he still was not troubling over what he was to say or how to meet the girl who thought him lying at the bottom of the sea. He was planning what he would take to Gail, and whether there would be time for him to get the evening train back to the shore. He was most impatient to find Dorothy and be done with the business.

It was a new servant who let him into the Stanford mansion, and calling cards were not among the articles he had remembered to order when he wrote his first letters for necessities.

"Is Miss Stanford at home?" he asked eagerly as he entered.

The man said that she was.

"Then please ask her if I may see her at once. I haven't a card with me."

Benedict was too much absorbed to realize that the servant would not know his name, and was not surprised when the man said yes, sir, and moved off without delay. In fact the servant had taken him for one of Miss Dorothy's friends who was there but the day before and sent up word to her that Mr. Walsh had called.

Miss Dorothy took her time as usual with her toilet. She was always one who made an effective entrance, and realized that a delay sometimes only made her coming more welcome.

Benedict sat idly looking about the great handsome room where he had spent so many weary hours waiting in the past. He drew a breath of relief that he was no longer under the bondage of fear lest when she came her mood would not be friendly. He realized with joy that he could look at the great mass of American beauty roses in a crystal bowl on the table without a pang of jealousy toward him who had sent them. Those were likely Briggs' roses. Poor fellow! What a lot of anxious hours he would have to spend there waiting for his erratic lady. But perhaps he was wronging Dorothy. Perhaps it was because she had not really loved him that she had treated him so. It might be that she really loved Briggs and would never turn from him to others. Well, be that as it might, he knew now as he sat in the old place waiting for her to come that he did not love her, and never could have loved her. He was impatient to be gone that he might go back to the shore that night.

It almost troubled him that he could have changed so. It seemed weak and wavering to have been so sure about her and now not to care at all, and yet, there were all those months, more than a year of them, that she had held him at a distance. While he tried to excuse himself it suddenly came to him that until Gail came into his vision he had never known his ideal, had never dreamed what a woman could be.

At last he heard footsteps on the polished stair. How often the sound had stirred his pulses. Not a thrill came to them now, only relief that at last she was near and he could have it over. It was going to be so much easier now that he knew of her engagement to Briggs. That made everything clear and plain and they could meet on a matter-of-fact friendly basis and let bygones be bygones in a most cheerful way.

He looked up to see her as she approached, a dainty figure in a striking gown of shimmering old rose, her head dropped sideways in the old attitude, her eyes beneath down-drooping lashes about to be swept upward in greeting. How often he had stood and watched for the second when she would look up that way to him, her dark eyes full of hidden mysteries, coquetting even in seriousness. But now as he rose to meet her he felt half impatient of the delay.

He stepped toward her, and her small white hand went out to meet his, and the eyes swept upward as was their habit, but there was no smile of welcome, no pretty deference, no easy moving forward to a chair after greeting. Instead she drew back as if in sudden fear and clasping her hands to her heart cried out, a ring of terror in her voice, her eyes large with apprehension, her whole attitude expressing consternation.

"Oh! oh!" she cried as if she could not take her gaze away, putting up her hands and pressing them upon her eyes to shut out the vision of him.

"Why Dorothy! Is anything the matter?" he asked coming nearer in astonishment. "Are you ill? Won't you let me help you to a chair? Shall I ring for a glass of water?"

He would have drawn her to a chair but she shrank away from him in horror, one hand upon her heart, her eyes wide and searching his face fearfully. "Why Dorothy, I don't understand. Won't you tell me what is the matter? I surely haven't startled you this way. You are not afraid of me, are you? I have only come to congratulate you on your engagement."

A scream from the girl's lips stopped his words, and she

turned as if she would have fled, but he caught her by the wrist and drew her into the room.

"See here, Dorothy!" he said suddenly comprehending, "I'm not a ghost. I didn't drown. I was saved and floated to shore. I'm perfectly alive and myself, and I've only come up to Washington for an hour or two to talk things over with you and get a few matters straightened out. You needn't be at all afraid of me. I've just come to tell you that you needn't feel at all embarrassed by the past. I feel that things are all right as they are."

But the girl had sunk into a chair and was shaking with sobs, her white face hidden by her hands, her whole small frame convulsed.

BENEDICT suddenly became aware of the mighty change that had taken place in himself. If this scene had occurred a year ago he would have wanted to take her in his arms like a little child and comfort her. The tiny curl in the back of her neck was strongly in evidence but it had no effect upon him. He was instead conscious of being annoyed that the business he had come for must be delayed in this way, and he stood looking down on her perplexed, and suddenly feeling his own bodily weakness, which until now had been held in abeyance by his own happy thoughts and his desire to get through and to get back to Gail.

Every instinct of manly courtesy demanded now that he do something to relieve the sufferings of the girl whom he had obviously frightened into a hysterical state, but in spite of himself he could think of nothing to do. What was there to do for a little creature like that in such a state unless you took her in your arms, and he had no right nor desire to do that. Indeed he felt a growing impatience with her foolishness and childish ways. Why couldn't she be a woman and sit up and behave, now that she was actually engaged to be married? What a woman for a man to make his wife anyway!

Gail would never have been so silly! Gail who drew him upon her raft and held him in her arms through the storm and wildness, knowing not yet whether he were dead or living! His heart quickened as he thought of her, and he sat down and tried to hasten matters.

"Dorothy," he said gently, "won't you listen to me? I haven't come to reproach you. I've only come to say it's all right. Don't you understand? I saw the notice of your engagement announced in the papers and came at once. I didn't want you to think I held any ill will."

"I thought you were dead!" sobbed the girl. "I did indeed. Everybody told me there wasn't any possibility of your being saved."

A cold chill crept to his heart. Was she going to claim him again in the old way and try to hold him? He frowned and drew his chair back a little, trying to think what was the best thing to say without being brutal in his frankness, but the childish voice went on:

"I was always fond of you, Clinton, you know, but nobody knew we were engaged, and you know how horrid and old I always look in black and Arthur had been pestering me for months."

Benedict drew back with a sudden relieved laugh, so natural and happy that the girl looked up from her applied weeping in astonishment and growing chagrin.

"Well, that's all right. Of course, Dorothy, when I was drowned you had a perfect right to call our engagement off and make what other arrangements you thought best. You needn't apologize. I'm glad you did it. In fact, I had already made up my mind before the disaster, even before I sailed, that you and I had made a mistake."

"No, Clinton, I was always very fond of you," sighed the girl, "only I was so young, you know, and it was so nice to have a good time before I settled down. And then it was so really hard to tell which one you liked best among a lot of nice men. You like one for one reason, and another for another, you know. Now I always did admire the way you comb your hair and the way you help a lady into a car. But Eddie Cady has perfectly lovely teeth and such good taste in flowers, and Arthur dances perfectly divinely."

"Is that the reason you have decided to marry him then?" asked Benedict contemptuously. Was it possible he ever found amusement in a childish creature like this? He half turned from her and stared out through the window into the familiar street. It almost seemed as though he had been translated into another world and were merely being permitted to look back now and see himself as he had once been.

"Oh, no, not altogether!" sighed Dorothy contentedly. "I don't know as I should have done it if you had been alive. You were always so charming too, you know, and let me do what I wanted to."

"Thank God I was not alive then," murmured Benedict under his breath.

"What was that you said, Clinton? I didn't hear. Why do you stay off there by the window with your face muffled in the curtains? I wish you would come and sit down and behave like yourself. What was that remark you made? You needn't be so savage."

Benedict turned quietly and came back to his chair.

"You cannot dance through your life," he said. "I was wondering what you are proposing to do after you are married if your choice of a husband rests entirely on how well he can dance."

Dorothy pouted.

"Now you are horrid. I don't like you when you talk like that. I didn't say I was going to marry Arthur Briggs merely because I'm engaged to him. I may change my mind before that time. Besides I don't see why I shouldn't dance through my life if I want to."

Benedict looked at her in a kind of hopeless contempt, which after all was more for himself and his former infatuation than for the silly girl.

"Well, Dorothy," he said, "I'm sure I've no objection to your dancing through your life if you want to, and I am glad you have found a partner to your taste. But if I were in his place I should not feel very well satisfied with an engagement that means as little to you as all that. However that's his business and not mine. I just came in to congratulate you and to say that you have my best wishes and all that sort of thing. I didn't want you to think that I'm going about mourning all my days, for I'm not. I've got bravely over my feeling for you, which I thought at the time was love, but which I have found out since was not, and I'm mighty glad you are engaged to Arthur Briggs."

"You're not going already?" said Dorothy tearfully as he rose. He had never acted like this before. She didn't know what to make of it. He was piqued of course and trying to bluff it out, and he really acted his part well, but it was not in her plan to let him go away like that. She never actually dismissed her followers. She liked to keep them her slaves through life and cast them a languid smile now and then, feeling what a thrill of might-have-been it gave them to bask in its transient light. She liked to have every man where she could call him to her bidding at a moment's notice. She liked to play one off against another who was a little too overbearing. And this one who had been dead and was alive again, and whose devotion had been the gossip of society for a year, this one she must keep at all hazards. Therefore she said tearfully, "You're not going already?" with the sweet reproach in her voice that had never before failed to put him just where she wanted him.

"Yes, I'm going," said Benedict cheerfully. "I've stayed longer now than I really meant to. I want to catch a train at four-thirty, and I've an errand or two before I leave the city."

"But you've only just come, and you've been almost dead. It's been terrible to think about your being dead, you've always seemed so—so kind of strong, as if nothing could ever hurt you. You surely will sit down for me when I ask you. I have a great many things to tell you. Let your errands go, and telephone them, and don't leave town today. I want you to stay."

"I'm sorry to refuse, but my errand is very important and it cannot be done by telephone, and I must leave town to-night."

There was a new hearty ring in his voice as if he were glad he must leave town tonight that made Dorothy sit up and take notice. She stared at him with a puzzled expression for a moment, this tall handsome man who had been her abject slave for so long and who presumed to order his times against her wishes. Then she tried her sweetest wiles. She drooped her lovely head, and her long lashes adorably fringed her softly flushed cheek.

"You don't love me any more," she said in a low, sad voice that trembled.

"Why, no, Dorothy, I don't," he said in a matter-of-fact tone. "In fact, to be perfectly frank, as I have told you, I don't believe I ever really loved you at all in the way I thought I did. I think it was all a terrible mistake which I'm glad we found out in time before it was forever too late."

There was something in his tone that was strangely chilling, but still she thought he was bluffing to lead her on.

"You talk as if you were saying good-bye!" she pouted.

"Why I am," he said frankly. "From this time our ways will have to part."

She was still a long minute, the kind of demure emotional stillness that had never failed before to work its mystery on the victim. Then she lifted the long eyelashes with coy shyness, a glint of tears in the eyes, a hint of a sorry smile about the charming lips, a lurking dimple in the lovely curve of her cheek near the corner of her mouth, lure in the very turn of her head, seduction in her very glance. She was staking her last chance.

"Don't you want to kiss me, Clinton?" she murmured

softly, tenderly, in the voice she knew he used to love and seek to provoke.

She lifted a little white ringless hand from which she had slipped Briggs' diamond a moment before, and held it out suggestively, with modest shyness.

It was one of those tense moments that she knew so well how to create, and that she seldom allowed to be too frequent in the experience of one man. She stood in breathless expectation and the very air of the elegant drawing-room seemed palpitating. Benedict drew sharply back and spoke with ringing firmness in his clear voice: "No, Dorothy, it wouldn't be right, and I don't want to!"

The girl looked up half frightened at his tone, startled into a question that afterward she wished she had not asked:

"Why?" There was lure in her face yet, and her voice was tender and innocent and grieved. No man had ever yet resisted that from her. It was her last resort; a tone which made a man feel that he had been cruel to her, made him feel like a beast who had misunderstood and trampled on a precious privilege. But Benedict answered instantly without embarrassment:

"Because you are engaged to another man, and because— I am in love with another woman! Good wishes and good afternoon, Dorothy!"

Without even taking her hand he bowed and went out from her presence.

Dorothy Stanford, petted child of fortune, stood still in the great room, her little hand fallen to her side rejected, the great bowl of costly roses behind her, and her gorgeous diamond flashing from the table by her side. But a strange cold fear was creeping into her silly little heart with the conviction that this strong, true man on whom she had leaned in spite of her follies, was gone from her forever! He loved another woman! How strange, how impossible, how calamitous it seemed!

She moved across the long room to the window as in a

dream. She drew the heavy silk curtains aside and looked out, watching him as he walked with strong quick stride down the street, walking out of her life into the life of another woman. Who was that other woman? How she hated her! And two real tears rolled down her cheeks and splashed their cleansing over her sinful little hands, two tears so small beside her childish guilt! So inadequate to wash away the stains of all the follies she had wrought!

Out into the clear autumn air and late afternoon sunshine walked the man with a buoyancy of step and a lightness of heart that he had not felt since he was a child. Despite his weakness he walked as if on wings. He was free of heart and might go to the woman he loved and tell her all his soul. He called a taxi and hurried away to the half past four train, rejoicing that he had not been delayed overnight. It seemed as though he had been away from her for weeks, and would have a great deal to tell her. Not much about the woman he had just left and his farewell to her, but volumes about his own heart life and his longing for her. All too slowly for his joy moved the wheels that carried him back to the cottage by the shore, and the dear woman whom he loved. He lay back and closed his eyes to rest, but he was not aware of his weakness or weariness. He did not even remember that he had taken no nourishment since noon, and had omitted his medicine since morning. His joy was bread and medicine to his soul, and for the time he needed no other.

It was late when Benedict succeeded in finding a boy to row him over to the Point. He was forced to go to a miserable little restaurant and get something to eat while he was waiting for the boy to find the owner of the boat and get the key. Yet the dirty little hole might have been a palace and the food nectar and ambrosia for aught he knew, so happy was he.

Seated in the boat at last with dim distant stars overhead and the quiet dark gray of the water beneath, and all about them the lap of the tide among the rushes through which they surged noisily now and then, he suddenly became aware of great weariness and a giving way of the forces that seemed to hold him together. He tried to pull himself out of the nervous tremor that had come upon him, but strange fears had beset him. Suppose she did not care for him! Suppose she resented his going away to Dorothy, as if he had not been honorable with her. Perhaps he should have told her his errand, or perhaps he ought to have just written Dorothy congratulating her and stayed with the woman he loved. And yet, he now felt that no written word would have been as final as the experience through which they had passed. Dorothy had done her utmost and he had not returned to his former feeling about her in the least. The utmost he had felt for her was pity and contempt. He despised himself for not having seen before how shallow and faithless she was.

As he neared the dark line where the cottages stood out a stark row against the gray void of the sea his fears increased. It seemed a year since he left that morning. Why had he not given Gail some little hint of how he felt, enough to insure him welcome on his return? What wild fancies were whirling one after another through his brain! He needed to get some sleep. Would she be glad to see him? Would she insist upon his going to bed at once, or would she let him sit up and tell her all that he wanted to say? Would the old lady and Corinne let them have a chance to talk by themselves, or would they have to wait until morning when they could go out to the sand by the sea?

Perhaps if she insisted on his going to bed at once she would come by and by and read to him, and then sit by his side and let him speak. He could tell her how he loved her. It wasn't the way he would have chosen. He wanted to tell her as a man would tell it, not as an invalid. Perhaps he would only ask her to hold his hand tonight and in the morning he would tell her. She would understand. She always had understood since first he had known her. She never had failed to look up with that answering smile and those eyes that knew his heart. And yet, he somehow had a feeling that things would be different. The old angel life was over. He had broken the golden cord that held them to that ideal life by his going away this morning, and it could never be quite the same again. But something better might come. It would have to be a test of whether she loved him or not. And now he knew that his soul was knit into hers, and that if she said no his life would be empty.

As they neared the rude little landing at the Point he strained his eyes to make out the cottage that stood alone by the sea. Yes, there it was with its weather-beaten gables outlined against the sky, and the boom of the waves and the toss of the froth blurring its front. But there shone no light from the west wing where his room had been. A dull disappointment spread over him, and he told himself he was weak and childish to care, for of course they would not be expecting him at this late hour. They would think him wise enough to stay in a comfortable bed in a civilized place and not run away to a lonely little house at the end of nowhere on a windy night like this, and he an invalid.

He almost laughed out in his eagerness as he thought of the look that would be in their faces when they saw him. Would the girl be pleased? She would not be expecting him now, for it was long after the hour for the trains. She would think when he did not come at the regular train hour he could not come until morning. He could tell by her face when he saw her what his fate was to be. He would not have to wait until morning. He would know at once by the lighting of her eyes whether she was really glad or not. If she felt as he did that they belonged to each other she would show it in her face. And how he would make up to her for having gone off in the morning without telling her what his errand was. He could see she was both hurt and troubled by it. But he would tell her and if she would let him he would never keep anything from her again.

He paid the boy and climbed out upon the wharf. The boy gave him a hearty thank you for the liberal amount he had received and pulled long strokes out into the gray water again and was soon lost among the rushes and the night. The lonely crickets chirped among the dry grass, and the sea boomed a funeral chant, but the man went forward with confidence toward the house where his loved one was. He knew that his lips even were trembling and that there was no strength left in his limbs, but it was only a few steps now and he would be with her and be comforted.

12

HE stumbled up the steps and tapped softly at the door. He did not want to alarm them, but no one answered until he had rapped twice. Then he heard Corinne's heavy footsteps thudding disconnectedly downstairs. Ah! That was why he had seen no light. They had all gone upstairs to bed. They had not expected him and they had taken Gail upstairs too.

After due consideration and a third knocking at the door, the voice of Corinne boomed forth in courageous alarm.

"Who all's thar, an' what yoh wants dis time o' night?"

"It is I, Benedict, Corinne!" he answered joyously. He felt like swinging his hat up in the air and shouting.

Corinne hesitated again and carried on a slight altercation with someone apparently upstairs, then she slowly drew back the bar that went across the door every night, and turned the key, opening the door a few inches and peering cautiously out into the night, revealing her head in its native state of many small alert pigtails bristling at intervals like a dark halo.

"Well, I'm back tonight, Corinne, as I promised," he cried joyously to reassure her. "Are the folks all gone to bed?"

"Great day in de mawnin'!" cried Corinne, "here's de sick-abed man got back, an' he ain't got de lady!"

"Aren't you going to let me come in, Corinne?" he laughed. "I'm cold and tired and hungry. I tried to get something to eat across the bay but it wasn't as good as your cooking."

"Bress my soul, Mist' Ben'dic', whar yoh done ben? Ain't you found de lady? What yoh done wid dat child? She was clean beat out takin' care ob yoh. Yoh hadn't oughtta come back an' lef' her. She ain't fit to do no wohk yet awhile. She needs res', she do. What yoh ben an' leave her do?"

"What do you mean, Corinne? I haven't seen any lady, not any lady that you know. I've been up to Washington and back today and I'm dead tired. I'm all in. Can't you open the door?"

"Great day in de mawnin', Mist' Clint'n, yoh don' mean to say you ain't seed Miss Gail whar yoh done ben?" She reluctantly opened the door and let him enter, but her tone had a threatening note and she stood with arms akimbo, in her ample flowered wrapper, surveying him with disapproval.

"Miss Gail?" he cried in alarm. "Why, where is she? No, I haven't seen her. Isn't she here? I left her down at the little wharf this morning. Didn't she come right back to the house? Haven't you seen her since? Haven't you done anything about it? Perhaps she is drowned."

He had come close to Corinne and seized her fat shoulder in a firm grip, now, as if he would somehow shake the information from her without waiting for her words.

But Corinne shook her head sadly and decidedly.

"No, honey, dat chile ain't drownded. She come back to de house all right an' 'tended like she et her dinnah, but yoh could see wid yoh eyes shet she wan't takin' no signature oh it. She jes' poke down t'ings, an' set an' look sad. I knowed it fore she comed in de house. She walk up an' down de san' an' she kep' puttin' her hankchuf to her yeyes, an' she look all white round de mouf. Den she go sit down in de san' while, an' presen'ly she cum up an' et her dinnah, an' den she say she tired an' gotta go lay down. But she ain't lay down. I hear her walkin' round like she pickin' up things, and movin' her feet like she sittin' at de desk, and presently she comes down the stair an' say she see some devertisements in de papah an' she gotta go get somepin' to do. She ain't scarcely got de words out 'fore long comes de grocery-boy an' long she go totin' with him spite all we all kin say. My, Mis' Battin she just cry hahd but it don't do no good. She gone. She say she don'no when she cum back."

"And you don't know where she is? She didn't leave any address?"

He reeled in his weakness and would have fallen, but Corinne suddenly looked at his face and reached out her strong arms to catch him.

"Bress my soul, yoh white as a sheet, honey man. Yoh pore chile. Yoh ain't got right well yet an' here I'se keepin' yoh standin' up talkin'. Yoh jes' take off dat obercoat an' lemme put yoh to bed. Yoh ain't fit fer gaddin' round de country. We can't let yoh git sick again. What Mis' Gail gwine say when she git back an fin' yoh sick-abed again? Here, yoh march in thar an' git inta bed while I go git yoh some hot milk. Yoh sho am white as a sheet."

Corinne tried to enforce her words but Benedict would not be put to bed. He sank into a chair with his face in his hands and groaned. What a botch he had made of things, to be sure, going away like that in the morning and giving Gail a chance to slip away. It was like his dream come true. He had dreamed thrice over that she was gone and he could not find her. But that was when he was weak and sick. He had forgotten the dream when he walked and talked with her daily. But now it had come true and she was gone, and perhaps he would never find her any more! And it was all his fault. He should have told her everything before he left. She had a right to know. He should have let her go with him as she suggested. It was her right too. She had saved him from the sea and he was hers and she was his. Oh, what had he done to his life now?

Corinne brought him the hot milk and made him drink it. He handed her back the empty cup and lifted up his haggard face.

"Well, now what had we better do first?" he said, his voice husky with weariness and feeling.

"Do, honey man? Dey ain't nutin' yoh all kin do dis night. Dey ain't nobody on de islan'; dat fishman went out fishin' foh dark, down to de banks. He won't come in foh three, foh clock inde mawnin'. Der ain't no boat to be had. We can't do nuttin' cep' pray. Yoh all bettah climb into yoh bed an' begin. 'Pears like we's got a mighty lot o' it to do— that ar bressed lamb all 'lone out in de worl'."

"I will call to the boy who brought me. Perhaps he will hear and come back," said Benedict springing up and rushing out into the night again, in spite of Corinne's loud protests that there was too much wind for anyone to hear and the boy would be too far away.

Out into the night against the sound of the sea he sent his fine clear baritone:

"Halloo! halloo! come back! help! come back! help! help! help!"

But only the sea answered with a dull boom of hopeless negative, and the crickets chirped dreamily on without a break.

He turned at last and plodded heavily back to the house, too spent to hasten. He was trying to think of something to do. He must rest, of course, to be ready for action in the morning, but he must get the situation thoroughly in hand before he lay down. He would not take off his clothes. He would be ready in case anything happened, in case she came late as he had done and got some one to bring her over, in case—he couldn't think of any other case. His brain was almost too weary to act at all. He had been through a long hard day and this crushing climax was almost more than he could endure.

"Have you been to her room?" he asked dully as he entered the house again and found the old lady sitting sadly with white face and trembling hands.

"No," said the old lady. "She came down so suddenly and told us. She had only a small bundle with her, just a few things lest she might have to stay overnight. Why should we go to her room?"

The man was already half way up the stairs with Corinne behind him, large-eyed and heavily eager.

In a moment Corinne lumbered down excitedly, puffing like a porpoise, her eyes very large, bearing a letter for Mrs. Battin.

The woman's hand shook as she opened the envelope and took out the letter and the money. Her eyes dimmed with sudden tears. What did all this portend? Had something happened to the girl who had grown so dear to them all?

Corinne handed her her spectacles and stood at her side holding the candle near so that she could read. Corinne held her breath not to interrupt the reading, and the trembling old voice read aloud:

Dear Mrs. Battin:

My eyes are full of tears while I am trying to write this letter, for it is going to be a goodbye letter and you have been very good to me, an utter stranger, who came to you with a heavy burden out of the sea.

I would like to stay with you awhile and try to make up to you for all that you have done for me and the one I brought with me, but perhaps some day I shall be able to come back and show you how grateful I am. I cannot say enough about the beautiful way you took us into your home and did everything for us as if we had been your own. There are no words to express my gratitude, and it looks very mean in me to run away this way, but the time has come for me to go and it is better that I should do so without making any fuss.

It would only be hard for us if I tried to say good-bye, and you could not understand why I must go this way, and I could not explain.

My heart is very tender over the way you put me into your dear granddaughter's place and let me use her things and gave me her clothes. I know how hard it must have been for you and I have tried not to use many of them so that they will be fresh and pretty for you to look at just as she left them. But I realized how you felt when you gave them to me and I have taken with me the few that I need now. Perhaps sometime God will send you again some one in need as I was, so I have left the rest of the things to be there for another girl to use when she comes. I could not feel right to take away with me more than a few that I shall need immediately before I can buy more.

I am going away, as I shall tell you when I leave, to find something to do to earn my living as I have had to do since my dear father and mother died. You need not worry about me. I am used to it and have never had any trouble in finding something to do. It will not be long before I shall find just the right place, and when I get things straightened out in my life and feel that I am in a position to do so I will let you know where I am sometime. You have been very kind to me and I shall never forget.

I am leaving just a little to pay for some of the expense we have been to you. When I can I shall try to do something more to show you how I appreciate all you have done for us. Will you please give ten dollars to Corinne and tell her I can never thank her enough for what she has done for me, and for the way she took care of Mr. Benedict when I was not able.

With a great deal of love, and praying that you may be very well and happy, I am your grateful young friend,

Gail Desmond

The candle was shaking in Corinne's hand and tears were falling fast like rain down black cheeks and white wrinkled ones alike when the reading was done, and it was sometime before Mrs. Battin could speak.

"Then she meant to go!" she said sadly. "She was a dear child, and I have lost another daughter!" and she put her handkerchief to her eyes.

"You may 'pend 'pon it, Mis' Battin, honey," said Corinne putting the candle down hard on the little sewing-table and standing with her arms akimbo looking like an immense flowered bedquilt in tears, "you may 'pend 'pon it dat ar sick-abed man had sumpin' to do wid dis yere. Dey musta had some kind ob a scrap, an' fust he runned off and den she runned off. He comed back kase he's a man, but dat poh li'l' chile, she can't come back kase she's a woman an' she's bleeged to ac' like she didn't ca'h 'tall. Gals hes to be mighty 'tickeler what dey does. She jes' can't come back an' so he's bleeged to go aftah heh. Mis' Battin, honey, yoh reckum he's got sense 'nouf to know dat hisse'f 'thout bein' told? Men's mostly mighty stupid, 'pears to me. Yoh reckum he do?"

Up-stairs in the room that had been hers, Clinton Benedict sat down to read his letter. It was the first time he had seen his name in her handwriting, and his heart leaped at the thought that she had sent him a message. He tore the envelope open nervously.

Dear Friend:

    The time has come for me to go away and find my place again in the world. I have read the paper and I think I understand what sent you in such a hurry back to your friends with the glad look in your eyes. I would have liked to stay and hear you tell it all, but it is best that I should go at once while you are away. I know that you will not need me any longer, for you will be with your dear friends who have already been too long without you. I thank God that I was able to take their place a little while when they did not know where you were, and I shall pray always for great blessings on you and all you love.

I have not been able all these beautiful days while you were getting well to thank you for what you did for me, nor to say how glad I am that your splendid life was saved and not thrown away for my poor one. I have never asked you much about yourself, but I know somehow that you have some big place in the world, just as I knew that you were a great soul when you turned back to help me on the ship and let go your last chance of life as if you had plenty of others. I feel it has been a privilege to have been able to wait upon you when you were helpless, and I shall always be glad that I know there is such a man on the earth as you. I had thought there were no more since my father died. He never thought of himself.

You will please remember to take your medicine and not to overdo, for the sake of your nurse who has tried to help you back to health and strength again. You have been like my child so long that it is hard to stop thinking for you, but I beg you will be careful until you are fully recovered.

And now, as we were suddenly brought together for a little while, so we have been swiftly separated and sent in opposite ways. I will not say good-bye, but God be with you.

Gail Desmond

He was as one stunned. With the letter in his hand he bowed his head upon it on the bureau. Every word seemed to have burned itself into his soul, but the only thought he could gather and understand at first was that she was gone, gone of her own will out of his life forever. She had not said she would come back. She had not hinted at ever hoping to see him again. She had written these words as final. The black death that had yawned in the sea seemed engulfing him again. For what purpose had she brought him from that death only to plunge him into it again? How was he to live without her?

Corinne, her face still streaming with tears, went stealing ponderously up the stairs a creak at a time, imagining she was walking like a sylph. She peeked in at the door to see if the mere man was going to know what to do, but she stole away again in awe when she saw his grief and her heart turned straight around in its allegiance.

"Pears like dat chile did a very cahless ac' runnin' off an' leabin' dat man-baby up dar 'fore he got rightly goin' on his feet agin. 'Pears like she mought 'a' waited an' not fit till he war able to bar it li'l' bettah. He all broke up, he is. I reckum he gwine be sick ag'in an' she not here to boss him. Dat's jes' like a woman, runnin' off when she's mos' needed. Ef she doan' come back tomorra she'd oughta be spanked. Say, Mis' Battin, honey, yoh go up-stairs an' try an' coax dat Mist' Clint' t' come down to bed. I'll get it all ready for him. You go, honey."

The wrinkled hand of the old lady laid gently on his head made Clinton Benedict start and look up with a haggard face. But when she advised bed, and told him nothing could be done until morning and he must have some rest or he would be worn out and could do nothing then, he stumbled to his feet and promised to go and lie down. It was then they discovered the letter addressed to the doctor.

"I will see him the first thing in the morning," said Benedict sadly. "It may be he will have some idea where she has gone, but it scarcely looks like it or she would not have written a letter."

Corinne patted his arm as he went by her into the bedroom, and explained that she had put hot-water bottles into his bed and he must look out and not get burned. He tried to smile and thank her, but the effort faded on his lips.

The household settled into quiet, but there was no sleep for anyone. Corinne on her bed in the back chamber, and

Mrs. Battin vainly endeavoring to sleep, lay and thought about the sweet girl who had that morning been among them and now was gone, where? Would they ever find her again? What was the reason she had gone? Had the two young people had a difference of opinion, and was it final? Tears had their way, and both pillows were wet. Neither remembered the day when they stood on the rainwet piazza and disputed whether the girl should be allowed to bring her unconscious charge to the house. They only remembered the days of sunshine and joy she had brought them, and the beautiful love story they thought they had been watching through all these weeks. And now, was it over forever? And the young man, how would he bear it? Would it put him back into invalidism again when he was just beginning to get strong?

Finally worn out with excitement they fell asleep.

The man downstairs could not stay in his bed. Tired as he was he rose and walked the room. He sat down in the chair she had used, and laid his hand caressingly on the Old Testament that lay where she had placed it the night before. As if he thought he might draw some consolation from it, he drew it toward him and opened it where it would. His eye feel upon the words she had read but a few evenings before:

"He shall call upon me, and I will answer him; I will be with him in trouble; I will deliver him, and honor him."

He closed the book sharply. He could hear her sweet voice speaking the words and it wrung anguish from his very soul. He softly pushed open the long window and stepped out upon the piazza. The night was crisp and cold and a sharp wind stung his forehead. He shivered as he stepped into the night.

The tide was out and the long stretch of beach gleamed wet and lonely in the dim starlight. The ocean tossed like a mad thing chained for the moment and harmless. Phantom lights gleamed fitfully at sea, and toppled out of sight. The surf had the air of being busy otherwise for a while.

Benedict stepped down upon the sand and walked along

the beach, his hands gripped behind his back, his face lifted up to the sky.

"O God," he cried in a voice that it seemed could only be heard by heaven, so set apart the time and place seemed to be, "O God, take care of her! help me to find her! I love her! O God, help me!" and falling upon his knees, the strong man bowed, praying, perhaps for the first time in his life.

How long he knelt he did not know. It was all very still and the tide was away and busy. He was kneeling in the very spot where last they had sat together.

After a time he got up and went back to his room. The candle was still burning fitfully with weird shadows across the wall. He saw the white gleam of Gail's handkerchief where she had dropped it by her chair, and stooping picked it up and laid his lips upon it. He knelt for a moment beside her chair with his head bowed against the faded flowered cushion on the back, then he got up and went to his bed, as if he had heard her voice telling him to do so. Vague sentences from her letter floated to him through his tired thoughts, and he lay down with her handkerchief against his cheek and slept.

It was dawn when he awoke and with his first breath he was conscious that she was gone. It seemed as if he had borne the burden of the knowledge of this fact for ages, and might for ages yet to come.

He started to his feet almost at once, aware that he must be up and doing. It had come to him in the night-watches that he must see the doctor first and then go to Washington and hunt for Gail. Surely she would be in Washington, and what were detectives for if not to find people when they were lost? She was no common girl; it surely would not be impossible to find her: and so hope stirred within him, and he rose and prepared to steal away without troubling his kind hostess and her weary handmaid.

Corinne however was already on the alert and had his breakfast steaming hot, and ready for him.

"De fish-boy jes' gone home fer his brekfus'," she whispered confidentially so that she would not waken the old lady. "He say he'll come back an' tote you ober to mainland in half an hour. Yoh ain't gwine find no folks up sooner'n 'at, so yoh kin jes' set down an' eat yoh brekfus' good an' right. Yoh can't go without eatin', an' yoh gotta keep up fer dat chile's sake. She's only a gal, yoh know. 'Pears like gals was borned to hab to be allus runnin' away when dey'd a heap rather stay behin', but yoh's a man an' yoh gotta fin' her, Mist' Clinton. Don't yoh nebber gib up till yoh fin' her. She's some'rs waitin' foh yoh to fin' her, so don't yoh get 'scouraged! She's breakin' her heart till yoh comes."

"You think that, Corinne? I wish I could," he said with a half smile, and sighed. "What did she run away for if she wanted to stay?"

"Cyan't yoh see dat, Mist' Clint'n, why yoh's mighty blind. Dat's plain ez nose on yoh face. She's jes' natchally bleeged t' run kase she's a gal, and yoh's a man an' has de pribilege of runnin' arter ef yoh likes."

"But she's left no trace behind her. If she had wanted me to find her wouldn't she have left her address?"

"No sah. Dat wouldn't hab ben runnin' 'way, dat would hab ben leabin' a trail behin' heh. No sah, it's up to yoh, sah; ef yoh wants heh yoh hez to fin' heh!"

"Thank you, Corinne; I'll find her if it takes a lifetime," he said, throwing back his head with that high look he had worn on the deck of the ship; and rising, he took his hat and coat and started, promising to send word the minute he had a hint of news and also to keep in touch with them daily.

13

WHEN the doctor opened his letter Benedict was startled and thoughtful as he saw the money which fell out. Fifty dollars! He could distinctly see five ten dollar bills. What did it mean?

In a moment more Doctor Phelps handed over the letter with a questioning look:

Dear Doctor:

I have to leave the shore quite suddenly without waiting to see you. I do not know what your bill is that I became responsible for, but I am enclosing fifty dollars, which is all I can spare just now, but later when I have secured a position I hope to get I will write you and find out how much I owe you.

It is a great disappointment to me not to be able to thank you personally for your kind attention during these weeks. You have been more than physician, you have been friend to a couple of strangers in a strange place, and there are no words to tell you adequately how grateful we are to you. I know that God will bless you for it, and we shall never forget it.

With grateful thoughts,

Gail Desmond

"Do you mean to tell me that Miss Desmond became responsible for my bills during my illness?" asked Benedict looking up suddenly, his eyes bright with mingled emotions.

"She did," said the doctor, bowing gravely, "but I didn't intend to take it myself. I was obliged to accept the fee for the specialist because I wasn't in a financial position to take care of it myself, and she insisted on taking no chances with your life. But I had no idea of accepting a cent from her on my own account, and if you will give me her present address I will return this money at once. It was a pleasure to be associated with a girl like that, and I count it an honor to have served you both in your time of need."

"I'm sure I wish I could give you her address," said Benedict fervently, "but I don't know it yet, and I'm not sure that I ever shall know it. She has gone and left no trace behind her. She has been like an angel to me, and her disappearance is almost as an angel's might be."

The doctor looked keenly at the young man, noted the haggard face and heavy eyes, and laid his hand upon the other's knee.

"Tell me about it."

With bowed head Benedict told him.

"Well, well, well!" said the doctor huskily, getting out his handkerchief. "She's a great little girl! She's the greatest little girl I ever saw."

"But about this money," said Benedict, suddenly aroused to a thing which was in his mind of secondary consideration. "You say she paid the specialist? How much was it, do you know? And weren't there other things she paid for? I've heard them talk about a nurse, although she isn't very clear to my mind. I guess I was about over the border there for a while."

"You certainly were," said the doctor with tears in his

eyes. "You had only the one chance, and that was the operation. Of course we didn't know that when we sent for the specialist. I thought you might pull through, you looked so strong. I was going to take the chance, for I hadn't the money to do anything else, and I didn't know whether you had."

"I have plenty," said Benedict quietly, as though it meant little to him, having always had it.

"Well, I didn't know of course; and then there was the responsibility of an operation. Somebody had to take that and you were a stranger. We could find nothing but initials. The little girl took the chance for you."

"I guess I owe her about everything I have," said the young man, deeply stirred. "She saved my life."

"I guess she felt it was a matter of a life for a life on both sides," said the doctor.

"Well, I owe her everything, and I don't know where she is. I have plenty, and from what little she had told me of herself she hasn't much of anything. Now what am I to do?"

"Oh, you'll find her. The world isn't so large as you think. Keep up your courage. But you'll have to take good care of yourself. No more sleepless nights like last night or you'll go down like a rush in the wind, and then who's to carry on your search? Now of course she may imagine she owes me something more, and write to me for a bill by and by, but from her letter I shouldn't expect that to be very soon, so of course we can't wait for that. Have you any idea where her former connections were? Would she be likely to go back? She mentioned two places, did she? Well, why not telegraph a minister or a doctor, or some town official in those places and see if they know her present address. Telephone? Oh, yes, of course that would be quicker, but long-distance phoning counts up, you know. Well, I'm glad you have plenty of money, young man; you'll get what you want all the sooner, of course. Money does make things move easier, there's no doubt about it. Have you any idea she's gone to Washington? It might be well to put a good detective to work. By the way, we'd better go right over to the station and see if they know what train she took. And who brought her over from the Point? The grocery-boy? Let's look him up at once. You have an hour before the Washington train leaves. Time enough to do a good deal of phoning. Meantime, while you call up that grocery-boy and get all the information you can out of him, I'll fix you some medicine. I don't like the look of your eyes. You haven't strength enough to go through all this yet. That little girl needs a trouncing. She ought to have put aside everything and waited until you were stronger."

"She thought I had gone to my friends, you know."

"Yes; well, she ought to have been sure before she took any such decided steps. Girls do get skittish now and then, the best of them, I know, and kick the traces unexpectedly. Well, she's the best girl I ever came across, and you're to be congratulated on finding her out of a whole universe full of silly shallow-pated creatures. Now you take this chair and call 191W, that's Kaylor's grocery, and ask for the boy who takes the afternoon order to the Point."

The grocery-boy didn't know anything about the young lady he had brought over to the mainland. He had gone directly to the store, and she had left him where he landed. He hadn't noticed which way she went. She walked slowly down the street behind him. He guessed she went to the station, but he didn't know.

The station-agent remembered her. He was sure she was the lady to whom he had sold a ticket to Washington for the afternoon train. She was the only lady who bought a ticket that afternoon, and he remembered her particularly because he had never seen her before. She wore a dark blue dress and a dark hat, and had big blue eyes and lots of hair.

Benedict drew a long breath and hope began to rise. Of course he hadn't found out much yet, for one would naturally go to Washington first unless one were going farther South. It was the nearest large city.

Next he called up Information and asked for connection with a minister in both of the cities which she had mentioned in her casual talk of home. As her father had been a clergyman it seemed likely that another one of the same denomination might at least have heard of her, and know someone who knew her. At least he would leave no stone unturned that might lead to a clue to her.

After much delay they finally succeeded in getting someone in one place who responded, but he declared at once that the young lady in question was drowned in the recent disaster of the Baltic, and when Benedict said he knew that she was not they said her name had been in all the papers, and there had been much sadness over it because of her father's past connection with that place.

The other call had not responded when Benedict had to leave for his train, but as he said a hurried good-bye he left in the doctor's hand a check which he told him he was to use in paying for the phoning, the remainder to supplement Miss Desmond's fifty dollars.

When the doctor looked at the check he saw that it was made out to himself for two hundred dollars, and he sat down in his office-chair and put his hands over his dazed eyes for a minute to get his breath. Fees like that didn't come his way often. In fact, he was having the time of his life, though he had to confess that he would give it all to know where that sweet-faced little runaway girl was at this minute.

In Washington, Benedict of course knew just what to do. In half an hour after his arrival he had a consultation with his lawyer and one of the best detectives in the country, and before two hours had passed the most elaborate and scientific system in the country had been set to work to find out Gail Desmond and bring her back to her friends. Not a thing that could be thought of was left undone, and no trouble or expense was spared to make the search as thorough as possible.

While Gail Desmond was trudging through the rain in

New York hunting for her place in the world that place was waiting for her. Eagerly and literally hundreds of people were busy at work trying to find her and bring her to it; and yet God had his plan to work out, and this was all a part of it, for the finding of Gail Desmond affected more lives than her own, and all is not lost that seems to be; neither are we at any time out of the sight and care of God who attends the sparrows on their way.

After he had set in motion every possible force to find Gail Desmond, one of the first things that Clinton Benedict did was to buy a Bible.

He had never owned a Bible in his life. Somehow his early training had been completed without that acquisition. He had gone to church when he liked, and had done very much as he pleased in most of the choices of life, and though Sunday school had been a part of his childhood routine he had never earned a Bible for reciting verses, nor had a religiously inclined relative ever given him a copy. He had read the Bible, of course, occasionally in church, or had heard it read, but never until Gail began to read it to him did it have a living vital place in his soul.

He had a strange feeling about that Bible when he went to buy it, an almost shamed feeling, as if it were a queer thing for a man to do to buy a Bible. He almost felt as if it were a sort of drug that he had come to depend upon that had suddenly been taken away from him and he found he could not do without. Perhaps it was not so much for the Word itself as for the memory of the sweet voice that used to read it, that he wanted it now; though the great thoughts had found pleasant entrance in his mind, and many passages had set him thinking in new lines. Moreover he felt that he would be nearer to the girl he loved if he had that book; for he might be reading some of the same words at the same time she read them, and it was comforting to think of it. At least it was loving the same things she loved.

As he stood shyly at the counter waiting for his Bible to

be brought he was surprised to find other people, sensible, well-dressed, thoughtful people buying Bibles, and acting as if it were an every-day thing to buy a Bible, like getting a hairbrush. It had always seemed to him that Bibles were property that one acquired at church, or that were indigenous to the home, and that getting them any other way was a sort of declaration of weakness.

One thing was sure, a Bible he must have, and so he bought one and went away with his precious parcel, feeling suddenly very rich.

As he was walking away from the book-store an automobile slowed up and a lady leaned out, bowing and smiling so noticeably that pedestrians turned and looked after the favored gentleman. Benedict looked up, recognized Dorothy Stanford, and lifted his hat, but his thoughts were so thoroughly engrossed that it did not occur to him to stop. He greeted her as he would have greeted any other acquaintance and passed on his way. But the car turned and whirled up to the curb at this side.

"Won't you get in and ride, Clinton?" called the girl, leaning over with the sweetest of smiles.

Benedict stopped, annoyed to be interrupted.

"Thank you, no," he smiled pleasantly. "I've only a few steps to go, I'll walk," and lifting his hat he went on.

The girl bit her lips in vexation and ordered her car away, but in her eyes there came a look that meant trouble. She thought she had seen in that haggard face and that haughty look the real truth, that Benedict was eating his heart out for her, and satisfaction filled her silly little self. It had piqued her to have him refuse the kiss she had offered. As she watched his tall shoulders disappear around the next corner she was nearer to loving him than ever in her life. Just give her a man who was hard to win and Dorothy Stanford was in her element. For the time being she adored him. And she thought she had seen that he was pining for her, and therefore she set herself to break his haughty indifference and bring him to her side once more. She would find a way even if she had to marry him after all. She wasn't sure but he would be better than Arthur, anyway.

Each morning early Benedict was on hand to talk over with the detectives any progress that had been made or any clues that had been found. And each day he tried to think out new ways of discovering what had become of Gail Desmond. When Mrs. Battin came up to her winter home he visited her there nearly every day or called on the telephone.

A week or two passed, and still there was no hint to tell what had become of Gail.

Dorothy Stanford was biding her time. She waited expectantly for the first great social event of the season, when she meant to get hold of Benedict and devote herself exclusively to him. To that end she selected her most stunning costume of the color that he used to like, and went to the party in her sunniest mood to set her project going. She arrived at the hour when she thought she could make the best impression, but when she looked about carefully he was not there. She waited all the evening, watching every new arrival, but he did not come.

The next day she called him up at his apartment and rallied him on his non-appearance, asking him to dine with her that evening. He replied pleasantly, "Thank you, but it will not be possible."

"How long are you going to keep this up?" she demanded teasingly. "You are acting like a naughty little boy who won't play because you didn't get your turn to be it."

"Dorothy, you misunderstand me. I have been very busy with important matters. I had neither the time nor the inclination to come last evening, and I am very content with matters as they are between us."

"What is the reason you cannot take dinner with me this evening? I want to have a long talk with you, and we should be undisturbed tonight."

"I have another engagement."

"Break it!"

"I cannot."

"Not for me?"

"No."

Dorothy allowed a long telling pause to ensue, and her breath came with a quick catch over the wire like a sob:

"You are very cruel!"

"No; I am not cruel."

"You are unkind!" An actual sob.

"No. But I have changed in some ways."

"I should think you had!" with emphasis, and Dorothy hung up with a click.

The engagement which Benedict had for the evening was to meet Doctor Phelps and take him to his club for the night. They had a long heart-to-heart talk that evening to their mutual benefit. The things they said, and some they did not say but both understood, about the sweet girl who had gone from them, eased the pain of both of them. Benedict forgot the momentary annoyance of Dorothy's persistence. To him she seemed more like a beautiful little humming bird who persisted in getting before his eyes. In his absorption he had for the moment lost sight of the real selfishness and treachery that lay concealed beneath her pretty exterior, which he had begun to suspect. She seemed so far removed from him now that he simply did not think of her unless she brought herself to his notice.

Miss Dorothy Stanford bided her time in sulky silence. She had been wont thus to punish Benedict when he overstepped any bounds she had set, and she thought now to use the same methods that had been so effective in the past. But the days went by, and still Benedict paid no heed, and Dorothy, sated with her betrothal teas and dinners and dances, and wearying of her betrothed, who in truth was a tiresome young man with altogether too much money for his good, determined upon some decisive action. She would find out once and for all whether this woman he professed to be in love with was a myth concocted to cover his pride, or whether she were a real flesh-and-blood rival. She had no doubt whatever even now but that she could conquer her former lover and have him again at her feet if she once set herself to the task. She had determined now to stop at nothing. She could brook no longer this continued indifference. He should yield to her charms and be her slave again; yes, even if she had to marry him. He was almost as rich as Arthur Briggs anyway, and twice as charming.

Since she could not bring him to come to her again by any device, she determined to go to him.

She took great pains to find out from Benedict's man through her own maid at what hour Benedict would be alone in his own apartments. The matter was transacted over the telephone, and the impression left that a friend, presumably a man, would call that evening. The maid discreetly hung up the receiver before Benedict's man had been able to discover the name.

Dorothy, alone, and charmingly gowned, arrived at Benedict's apartments only to be told that he had been called to his office on important business and would not be back until late that night. The servant, of course, had no idea that the unknown lady had anything to do with the man who was expected.

The girl was somewhat taken aback at the idea of visiting a business office alone at night, but only for a moment. She reflected that her advantage would be all the better. He could not well get away from her, and they would be less likely to be interrupted.

14

THE elevator was not running at night, and she had to climb to the seventh floor, which almost dashed her enthusiasm. She was quite white and drooping from the unusual exertion, and found it no task to produce the effect of fright and exhaustion when she paused at last and tapped timidly at the door that bore his name. He had taken her there once a year and a half ago to show her his quarters. She could remember his eager face, and her own bored attitude. She had not been interested in offices.

When he opened his office door questioningly she was all ready with her neat little explanation.

"Oh, Clinton, are you really here? I'm so frightened! And I was so afraid you would be gone."

She drooped and expected him to catch her, but he stepped back and flung his door wide open, making no attempt to assist her.

"Dorothy!" he said severely, "what in the world are you doing here at this time of night?"

Dorothy dropped into a chair and put her hand to her heart while her host remained standing in his open door regarding her. He was not going to be nice and help her. She must make the best of it.

"Oh, I am so frightened and out of breath. I had to climb those horrid stairs. I couldn't make the elevator-man come."

"The elevators do not run in this building at night," he said coldly.

She was not getting on very well.

"You see I started for Aunt Augusta's. Aunt Augusta has been taken quite ill and wanted me to spend the night with her, and father and mother are away. But when we got to Pennsylvania Avenue I found I had left my bag at home, and so I sent Thomas back for it in the car. It is only a block or two, and I thought I would like the walk, it is such a lovely night. I never thought of being afraid until Thomas was gone and I started up the side street past this building, and then I suddenly realized that a man was following me. I was so frightened I started to run, and once I almost fell. I saw your light up here and thought if I could get up here you would take me to Aunt Augusta's. I never was down in this part of the city alone at night before. I didn't know how dreadful it was. I shouldn't think it would be safe for you to stay here at night along. Someone might murder you."

"It is quite safe for a man, but it is no place for a woman alone at night," he said coldly. He was annoyed with her childish thoughtlessness, and he more than half suspected her of falsehood, for he was nearly certain she could not have recognized his window from the street. His mind was absorbed with other things and he did not want to be interrupted, for he had that evening received a telegram from the detective office in New York calling him there to follow a new clue.

"I was so upset," she murmured, sweetly, ignoring his coldness, "and so glad to get this refuge. This dear old office!" she added fervently, looking around with a languishing glance, "how well I remember the first time you brought me here. Do you remember, Clinton?"

There was that in her voice which used to stir him to the depths of tenderness. Now it wrought in him a fine impatience

It was so unforgivable in himself that he had ever thought he cared for this vapid little thing.

"Would you like me to telephone for a taxi?" he asked politely, moving toward the telephone.

"Oh, no; not yet," she cried with her hand on her heart again. "I'm so upset I couldn't go down those horrid stairs, I'm afraid. I haven't been feeling at all well lately. The doctor says I'm all run down and need a rest. He says I've been overdoing."

She watched him furtively to see what effect this would have on the stern visage before her. He had been wont to be solicitous for her health and welfare.

"You will not need to walk down," he said politely; "I can find the janitor and get him to run the elevator down for you. I should think if you're not feeling well you ought to get to your home or your aunt's at once and lie down."

"Oh, Clinton," she said coaxingly as she saw him reach toward the phone again, "won't you take me to Aunt Augusta's? I couldn't stand it to be alone in the dark even in a cab just yet. I'm quite unnerved. I feel as if I were going to faint when I get frightened like that, and the doctor said it was really quite dangerous for me to get like that."

Benedict had already gone to the phone and taken down the receiver.

"Just a minute, please; I'll see if I can't fix things," he said pleasantly, though his brow was perplexed and anxious.

He called up a number and the girl watched him furtively, wondering what he was going to do.

"Is this the club? Is that you, Johnston? Well just run into the dining-room and see if Mr. Briggs is there yet. Yes, Briggs. If he's there ask him to come to the phone. You say he's right there? Yes, I want to speak to him. Hello! Is that you, Arthur? Glad I caught you in time. Miss Stanford has been badly frightened and taken refuge in my office. Yes, Dorothy Stanford. Yes, she was on her way to her aunt's on Eighteenth Street, you know, and her maid went back for something and a man followed her. No, she wasn't hurt; just badly frightened; but of course she oughtn't to go on alone, and I unfortunately have only a few minutes before I must go to my New York train, which I can't possibly miss. I'm going in response to a telegram on very important business. Come over and help us out, won't you? I don't like to leave Miss Stanford alone here with the janitor. You can get over in five minutes, can't you? Yes, I thought so. Thank you. Sorry I have to be so abrupt. You understand a train won't wait, and I simply can't miss it."

He hung up the receiver and turned about to face the angry girl with a face as calm as the one he had worn on shipboard when he saw the last life-boat drifting away from him.

"I'm sorry to seem discourteous, Dorothy," he said gently, "but I have but ten minutes to get some things in my desk and leave a note for my stenographer. You will excuse me if I go on with what I was doing. Arthur was at the club when I left and I knew he would likely be there yet. He will be down at once and take care of you. Won't you take the easier chair?"

Dorothy Stanford stood in the middle of the office dumfounded. For the first time since her babyhood days she recognized that her power over mankind had been thoroughly set aside and her wishes overridden by a man. Her eyes were blazing, her cheeks were crimson, her lips had gone white with anger. Her little drooping mouth took on an ugly curl that reminded one of the snarling of a wildcat.

"Clinton Benedict!" she said in her low-pitched voice, which fairly chilled with its coldness and hauteur, "I don't wish to go with Arthur Briggs, and you know it. I wish to go with you. I have something to say to you and I must say it. Take down that receiver and call up Arthur again and tell him you have found you can take me yourself. You know you just did it because you're miffed that I chose him instead of you. Tell him not to come. I simply won't have him. I'll run away and leave you to face him alone."

"Dorothy, what does this mean?"

He was standing gravely surveying her, his face stern, his voice solemn. She thought he was searching her face to see if there was hope left that she did care for him. She decided to venture a little farther.

"Call up Arthur and stop his coming and I will tell you," she said, melting into dulcet tones and looking unutterable things from her inscrutable eyes.

"I cannot, Dorothy. He has already started. He will be here in a minute or two."

The girl turned a frightened glance toward the door, then took a step nearer to her companion and spoke in a low tone:

"Oh, Clinton, don't you know what I mean? Don't you see that I love you? It is you I love, not Arthur. If you will take me away before he comes, I will break my engagement with him and will marry you."

"Stand back, Dorothy!" he ordered in tones of righteous severity; and he stepped away himself. "Sit down. You do not know what you are saying. You are indeed unnerved, Dorothy. I want no wife who comes to me in any such way. I could not trust you even if I loved you, and I have told you before that I do not love you. I belong to someone else, and while the world lasts you could never be anything more to me. Sit down over there, please. I hear Arthur coming. Excuse me. I will go and call the janitor to start the elevator."

He went out and left the trembling, angry, baffled girl alone. His crisp footfalls echoed down the marble hall and rang in the arched marble silence of other floors, and each sound was like a knife going through her heart. For the first time in her life she was experiencing some of what she had given to men since she was a child, because for the first time she had seen what a real true man could be. She had tested him and found him strong. There was such a thing as real love and integrity and purity in man. She knew it now, and knew that she had lost forever the one man of her acquaintance who she was sure possessed them all.

15

WHEN Gail awoke the sky was gray and there was a drizzle of rain.

"So much for my prospects of a bright morning after a dark night," she said grimly to herself. "But never mind, I'm going to make it bright. I'll get a job today. I must. I'll take anything."

On other mornings Gail had knelt a minute in prayer for a Guiding Hand to lead her. This morning she was so full of haste and determination to succeed that she hurriedly swallowed her sandwich as she dressed and started out. The girl at the desk in the employment office shook her head as she passed through and looked inquiringly. No, nothing had come in yet. She thought there might be something by and by.

Gail closed the door carefully and went out. She had a feeling that she would never likely come back there again. She carried with her the little bundle of things she had brought from the seashore. The day before she had washed out a few things and dried them as best she could over the radiator, pulling them smooth in place of ironing. She was prepared to go forth to whatever was in store for her.

She started down a street she had never gone before, with little idea of where she was going. Now and then she turned a corner, looking at the windows, always searching for a sign of help needed. She came on several cards hung out "Boy Wanted," and twice she went in to see if a girl wouldn't do as well, but was answered in the negative. Once she saw a sign announcing, "Girl Wanted, experienced." She went in, but they would not let her try. She set her white lips firmly, almost bitterly, and went on. She turned several corners and found herself quite bewildered about the streets. She had almost made up her mind to question a policeman when a card in a small dirty window caught her eye. "Stenographer wanted." A sign on the door read: "Ray-See Film Co. Studio."

For a second she paused as the thought came to her, What would her father have said about his daughter working in a place like this? But she shook it from her mind impatiently, for must she not have something? and she would be only a clerk anyway. As she laid her hand on the knob to go in, she had a feeling that she was about to do something momentous. She turned to look back at the street and the rows of dirty brick buildings that represented to her the cruel unfeeling world that had repulsed her so often during the last weeks. As she looked, two blocks away, she saw a tall young man swing from a crosstown car and walk toward the place where she was. Her heart gave a leap, for the figure reminded her of the tall young man she had nursed down by the sea. For an instant she thought perhaps he had followed her to New York. But immediately she put the thought out of her head and laughed bitterly at herself for being so foolish. Of course Clinton Benedict could not trace her in this great city, and probably he did not care to if he could. She flung a last defiant glance at the forbidding brick wall and went into the studio and a moment later Clinton Benedict with drooping discouraged mien hurried past the building.

The place was small and dirty and bare. Two desks

occupied a corner which was fenced off for an office, and a girl with a scant black satin sleeveless dress was pounding a typewriter. Her hair was cut short and oiled, a sleek ring plastered out on each cheek. She stared woodenly at Gail when she entered, and instead of answering her question, called in a nasal twang, "Mistah Fahley! Mistah Fahley! Here's somebody wants you."

Two men stood within a doorway just beyond. They turned at the call and looked sharply at Gail. They they both came forward, their bold dark eyes upon her appraisingly, noting her classic features with approval. They were both rather sporty-looking men, dressed loudly with flashy neckties and elaborate scarf-pins. One was in his shirt-sleeves, the other wore a derby on the back of his partially bald head. Gail did not like their appearance, but she was in no position to be a respecter of persons. She saw they were interested in her, and if there was a position of any kind that she could fill she meant to do it.

"You want a stenographer?" she asked, a trifle of dignity perhaps in her voice on account of the bold familiarity with which they looked her over.

"Well, not exactly, now; we just got that position filled." The man was still looking her over as if she were some kind of an exhibit at a fair.

"Oh!" Gail's face fell, and she could not help the distressed look coming into her eyes. They were large eyes, and very speaking.

The man looked pleased.

"We got another job you might fit into though p'raps. What d'ye think 'bout it. Bob? Would she do?"

"Bob" nodded not too eagerly, with his eyes squinted half shut.

"Might," said Bob succinctly. "Got good hair?"

Gail looked at the man as though his mind was wandering.

"He means have you got long hair," explained Farley. "We gotta have somebody with real long hair to take a part in a picture. The girl that had the part run away last night with one of the camera men, and we gotta fill her place right away. The whole picture's nearly done, except two scenes she was in. Now we gotta do all of hers over again. There's only five of 'em. It's good pay if you can do it. Ever do any movie actin?"

Gail shook her head. She knew very little of the world, but she felt instinctively a shrinking from having anything to do with these men. Nevertheless there flashed to her mind her determination to win in this fight for her life. She forced down her natural instincts and went on with the interview. Of course these men were coarse and crude, but perhaps they were good-hearted, she reasoned. They did not look unkind.

"What d'ye think about it, Bob?" asked Farley. "Think she'll do?"

"Lemme see her hair," growled Bob.

"Yes; take down your hair, Miss. Put your hat there on the desk."

Gail with her face flaming and an uncomfortable feeling that her father would have rushed her out of this place, and her mother would have wept at the thought of it, nevertheless took off her hat and pulled the pins out of her abundant hair. It was only a matter of business, of course, of whether she would do for what they needed in the picture, but it went sorely against the grain to stand up before these men and let them discuss the length and luxuriance of her hair.

As she drew out the last pin she turned her back to the men, shaking out her wonderful hair to its full length.

"Say, you've got plenty, ain't yuh, girlie? She'll be a peach all right, don't you think so, Bob?"

The man called Bob stood silent and dissatisfied a minute or two.

"You say Kittie won't take the part?"

"No, she's up in the air. Says she won't be a sub again. She's a star or nothing."

"H'm! Well, then, I s'pose there's no choice. We got to get that picture done. Try 'er out," he growled as he swung away into the other room.

Gail was trembling as she gathered her long locks into a coil and put in the hairpins. Should she go on? At every step her instinct was to flee the spot, but a voice seemed to remind her constantly that she would again be left to tramp the streets homeless and starving. She did not stop to analyze the voice or find out whence it came. In a moment more her hat was on and she was facing her would-be employer again.

"We'll pay you five dollars a day if you suit," went on the man as if he were pretty well satisfied with her appearance.

"Five dollars a day!" Gail gasped. It seemed as though she had found a gold-mine.

"Of course you have to furnish your own costume," enlightened the man as if that were a small matter.

Gail's face went down again.

"Oh!" she said dejectedly, "I'm afraid I wouldn't be able—"

"Why, you look all right just as you are for this film. You could wear those things in every scene except the second. There you'd have to have a kimono."

"When do you want me to begin?" said Gail, still half frightened.

"Right away!" said Mr. Farley. "This bunch has been waiting a half hour already. We hafta pay 'em fer the time. We just got word the other girl skipped. Camera man has no end of a temper on, so you better work lively and do what you're told."

"But I don't know what to do. Won't I have a chance to rehearse or anything?" Gail hung back.

"We'll tell you what to do, and how to look. All you have to do is obey. We're goin' to put you through a stunt or two now to see how you take."

Gail followed him fearfully through the door down a

dark passage and into a big room beyond where a lot of people were all chattering and lounging about in curious costumes. He introduced her to a tall lean man with a worried wrinkle between his eyes and left her there, going back to the office with Bob, who had beckoned him.

"Say, Farley, you're pretty rash, hiring kids like that for an important thing like this we've got on hand. She ain't an actor; she's a highbrow. Don't you know she'll spoil the whole show when she gets onto that second act? You'll have her kicking the traces and away, money or no money. She's an innercent, she is; but she won't stand for monkey shines, and you know what Charmer is."

"Now, Bob, that's right where you make your mistake. She may be an innercent, and she may be a highbrow all right. I grant you that. But that's why I hired her. Don't you know that's just the kind to make the picture more true to life? She won't be actin' and she won't need to be. She'll just be actin' natural. I've seen that kind before. They ain't common an' when you find 'em yu better freeze onto 'em, fer you won't see another in a life-time. She may kick at the second act. I hope to goodness she does. But she won't kick till the picture is taken. I'm goin' to run her scenes through—all but the one in the second act. Then we'll do that last, and she won't even have to see the rest of the picture at all. I'll tell Charmie to go easy till he comes to the very last minute, and then if there ain't some real actin' I'll eat my hat. She'll kick all right. Let her kick. She'll run from Charmie's arms as if he were poison, and Bob, isn't that just what we want her to do?"

Bob's eyes were growing narrow, and his loose heavy lips were relaxing into a half grin.

"All right. Go ahead. Pull it off if you can, but it'll take some work to do it. Better not tell her the whole tale at first, or you'll be in the soup."

"Not on your life, I won't," grinned Farley. "I gotta beat it now and see how she takes."

Meanwhile Gail had been sent upstairs to a large room lighted by a sky-light and filled with scenery. She was ordered to walk back and forth in front of the camera and bow and smile. She was told that she was being tried out to see if her face would photograph well. After this was over the command came to sit down and wait.

Soon the rest of the company drifted up, and as Gail waited among the motley crowd, a disturbance was suddenly created by the entrance of a thick-set coarsely handsome young man, who was hailed with delight as "Charmie." He was introduced to Gail as Mr. Archie Charmer. She discovered that he was the star of the play, and much sought after by every lady in the company. His ways were altogether too free and easy, and his voice was too loud to please Gail, who could not help thinking of the contrast between him and Benedict. Unconsciously she lifted her head haughtily when he looked her way, thereby calling upon herself the scorn of Kittie and Flossie, two of his strongest admirers. The man himself was not accustomed to such treatment from fair ladies, and this one was fair indeed. He liked it not. But he knew where his revenge could be had, and he bided his time, for he had been well warned about this newest member of the cast. He would show the lady by and by.

Before long Mr. Farley came out of the projection-room and spoke a few words to the camera man. Then he called to Gail and began to give her most explicit directions about every move she was to make. She assumed from this that her test had been successful, and did as she was told. She thought she was being rehearsed for the picture, and when the director told her to look out of a window at a certain spot as if it were an old friend, she did her best, having no idea that her picture was being taken all the time. The man told her to imagine herself a stranger in a strange land looking out of the window at the sea in the distance. He told her to think of it in its most beautiful moods. The expression that came into her face then must have satisfied him, for he nodded his pleasure at Bob who hovered in the background watching the latest actress with interest. Yes, she would do. She had the artistic temperament, the dreamer's face. Her eyes were large and tender and faraway, and there was no sense of self-consciousness in her face as she turned at last at the director's command and stepped away from the window. She had thought she was being tried out, but the record of her testing was safely on the film for the introduction of the picture.

The work went forward then with great rapidity. Gail was not required to be in the acting constantly, so she watched the others, and by the time she was called upon to come through a door and sit by a table reading a letter which contained sad news, and which brought her great distress, she was quite ready to enter into the spirit of the play as if it were a game she was playing with them. If she had not been so faint from lack of food and the excitement of it all she would almost have enjoyed it. It rather startled her that she had to be made up, but then it was all a part of the play and she submitted, astonished at the difference a little grease-paint made, how it coarsened the expression of her face. She did not like herself as she saw her reflection in the mirror, but she remembered that of course it would come off easily, and when she thought of five dollars that was to be hers that evening it did not seem to be an important matter.

The play itself seemed to be a simple little affair, with quite a moral attached, as Farley outlined it to her briefly, giving her pointers in the dressing-room and putting her through her motions two or three times before she went out to take her part.

Gail did well, though indeed much of her part consisted in looking sweet and sad, or sitting quietly apart from the others with a book, now and then looking up, but most of the time keeping in the background, a silent foil to the acting of the others. Her hardest part was to go through the act where she applied for position as companion and lady's maid to the silly "Flossie," but her recent experience in hunting employment served her in good stead, and she had merely to go through what she had been doing for the last two weeks. She did it so well that Farley whispered to Bob, "We gotta keep her. She's got good stuff in her. She's the kind that catches the pious people. Give the tip to the company, and don't let any of 'em play any tricks now. We'd sure be in a pickle if she beat it."

16

GAIL went out at the noon resting-time and spent her ten cents for milk. It seemed to be the greatest amount of nourishment she could get for her money, and she felt too weary and excited to eat. Besides, Farley had looked after her anxiously as she left the office and asked her to come back a little early; he wanted to coach her. In fact, he felt a little uneasy about her, lest after all she might escape him. He saw she had not enjoyed the company's boisterous familiarity, and by instinct knew that only the direst necessity would have brought her into their midst. She had the face of a girl who had always moved among cultured people and lived a guarded life.

When the outside air blew in her face again and she knew she was free, she wanted to run away, anywhere so that she would not have to return among those people who seemed so utterly alien to her.

But then she thought again of the money she must earn and reasoned with herself if she left now she would make the company a great deal of trouble now that her face was registered for the play. The work would all have to be done over again.

The afternoon's work was tiresome because there were several mistakes made and some scenes had to be done over and over again. Gail's head was aching, and every nerve seemed ready to jump out of her body. She looked around her at the other actors, their coarse faces perspiring from the heavy foul air of the place, their figures sagging with weariness. She wondered if it could possibly be true that many young girls yearned to become moving picture actresses. She had heard that often. If they could only see this place now, she thought, and know how hard they all worked, and how tired they were. But she tried to keep a calm face and go through her simple part as it should be done. She saw a look of approval on the face of hard old Bob as she made a particularly happy climax to one scene by turning back and smiling as she went out a door. Gail's smile was something worth looking at, and the keen picture man realized it.

"She'll make a hit with the audience if she smiles like that!" growled Bob with a grim smile.

"What did I tell you?" said Farley. "We'll have to keep her. I wish we didn't have to go through with that second act."

"Well, you do!" thundered Bob. "I thought you wouldn't have the nerve to carry it through. What if you've spoiled this whole day's work by sticking us with that little highbrow aristocrat?"

"Don't you worry, now; it'll be all right, Bob. Beat it now and leave her to me."

Gail had to ask that night for her first day's wages. Bob had advised Farley not to pay her until her part was finished, or she might yet slip away from them and spoil another day's work. Gail felt humiliated beyond expression to have to confess to the man how badly she was in need of money. When he heard her his eyes narrowed and he said shortly, "I'll see if I can fix it."

He retired into Bob's private office and told him of Gail's request.

"She must be up against it or she never would have taken the job at all, you can see that. But she's a dandy, an' we got to keep her."

Bob frowned.

"If you pay her all she's earned she's liable not to show up tomorrow."

"No, you're wrong there, Bob. She's this kind. If you give her her pay and tomorrow's too, she'll feel she's got to come back an' earn it. You just make an honest innercent like that feel under obligation an' you can do anything with 'em. You mark my words!"

Bob fairly exploded.

"Listen here, young feller, you can't expect to pick up a girl from nowheres off the street and trust her with the comp'ny's money. You wasn't born yesterday."

"Now look here, Bob, I'm not partin' with any long green without cause. I know what I'm talking about. You leave it to me. This kid's not goin' ta skip, an' to show you I know my oats I'm willin' to make it my own kale."

"Help yourself," said Bob, with a look of utmost scorn as he turned back to his desk. "Take care of a dozen charity infants if you want to."

When Farley returned Gail had worked herself into a frenzy of fear that he would refuse. Perhaps she would not be paid until she had worked a whole week. What could she do!

"S'all right, girlie. If you're up against it we'll be glad to help you out. We treat our folks fair. How much would you like? Ten dollars do?"

"Oh," gasped Gail, "I don't need so much as that. Five would be plenty, or even two or three."

"Never mind, that's all right," he urged, "you might need it. You are going to earn the rest tomorrow, aren't you? Well, just take it now. So long. See you in the morning, eight-thirty sharp. Just leave me your address before you go."

Gail thought quickly, a little sob rising in her throat at the thought that she had no address to give that she could call her own. She murmured "Y.W.C.A." half under her breath.

"Right; g'night."

The bewildered girl seemed suddenly too exhausted to think clearly as she moved out of the office. Her limbs were like lead. At the nearest restaurant she dropped into a chair and said weakly, "Something hot, please."

Even when she reached her narrow room she crawled into bed too weak to think or to worry about anything. She only knew that she must get to that studio again in the morning and earn the rest of the money she had taken.

When Gail awoke in the morning she began to think over the events of the previous day. She was not pleased with her new position. Her conscience did not dwell easily on the thought of her father's daughter being a moving picture actress. But, she thought, what could she do now? For she had taken the second day's pay and the night before had in a moment of terror of being homeless again, paid for her room a week in advance. It had eaten into the second five dollars so that she could not now return it. Besides, there was the picture. It would spoil four scenes if she did not return. And anyway, if she could return the money what would she do for a job again? These thoughts hurried her on her way to the studio.

It soon appeared that the black-eyed Charmer was the handsome villain of the play, brother to the heroine Flossie whose companion was Gail. It was after lunch that Farley handed Gail a kimono and a pair of slippers and explained to her that this Charmer was supposed to be enamored of her, and that her part was to hold him haughtily at bay, repulsing his every effort at acquaintance. It all sounded very simple and harmless as he told it. She smiled gravely and told him she thought she understood. In her heart she was saying that it would be difficult for her not to look too coldly at the great coarse, conceited creature.

The act began in her lady's boudoir, where she went through the various offices of arranging her lady's hair, and settling her comfortably on a couch with a book and a light. Then Gail's part was to be dismissed and leave the room holding a candle so that the light would shine full on her face, making a lovely focus first on her profile and then on her front face. She was to go to her own darkened room, set the candle on her dressing-table, deliberately let down her hair in front of the mirror and brush it out. Then she was to fling herself down on her couch and, after an attempt to read, seem to fall asleep.

The villain was to be concealed behind a curtain in the corner of her room, and from time to time show his face as he watched her. At a given signal she was to hear a noise and waken to find him stealing out from his shelter, when she would administer a rebuke and order him from her room, locking the door securely behind him. These were her orders. She did not in the least relish the performance, but she meant to do it as well as she could, knowing that if it did not have to be done over she would be done for the day.

She had no thought that there would be anything in the act to which she could object. Everything so far had been conducted most decorously, at least so far as she was concerned. There had been some things on the part of the other actors that she did not like, but she felt that it was in her own hands entirely how such a scene as this would come out, and she thought that she understood fully just what the manager wished. She had no fear but that she could do it. The last two weeks had given her plenty of practice in repulsing bold glances. She set herself for the act and did her best.

There was a peculiar silence in the room when the delayed second act began. Perhaps "Charmie" had whispered it around how he meant to have his revenge. Perhaps the other girls were jealously watching to see how the favorite would be treated by this haughty green hand. There was an tagonism among them all. She felt herself one against the whole company. Only Farley seemed to be friendly toward her, and him she watched as she went through her part, satisfied if he looked pleased.

Gail was very lonely when she entered the door of the darkened room with the candle-light on her face and one hand resting for an instant on the door-knob; lovelier still as she stood before the mirror at the dressing-table and held her hand around the candle-flame for a second so that the light was focused in the glass. Her hands were beautiful as they moved rhythmnically down the length of her wonderful hair, leaving shining smoothness in the wake of the silver-backed brush they had given her. She was deliberate in all her movements, even pausing for a moment and listening as if she thought she heard some one in the closet, holding the heavy waves of her hair back from her face, and letting the big sleeve of the kimono slip back and show the curve of her white elbow. The watching, jealous girls were surprised that she knew how to be so graceful. Even they could see her charm and resented it. They resented the approval on the faces of Bob and Farley. The new girl was making a "hit."

Gracefully she threw herself upon the couch at last, her long hair falling back over the head of the couch and to the floor in shining waves lit by the flicker of the candle. Anything more natural and lovely than her position as she lay asleep could not well be imagined.

Up to this point all was going well. Everything had been planned, and now the villain was stealing forth from his hiding-place so silently, so cautiously, that he stood almost over her, and yet she had not heard the signal nor suspected.

Suddenly some inner consciousness gave her warning, some sense of the nearness of a hateful thing. Was it a hint of liquor and stale tobacco on his hot breath as he stooped nearer? She only knew that the time had come to act. She forgot that she was to wait for a signal, she forgot that she was acting, or that there was to have been a signal at all. A higher signal had been given than ever Farley could control, and she sprang to defense.

No practiced acting could have been more perfect than the way she lifted up her head and gazed in horror at the wild, loathsomely handsome face as it bent over her, the whole look repulsive in the extreme.

One instant only she gazed as if under some terrible spell. Then all the righteous wrath of her Puritan ancestors rose in its might and stood forth in her face. The lights in her eyes were like the lightning darts of an avenging angel, the fine flame of her face was fanned from her pure soul. With all the strength that was in her she struck out at the man, and from that instant on the scene became real. There was no more acting. The director held his breath and stepped back. Bob puffed his heavy flesh into red swaths about his chin and breathed as if he had an apoplectic fit, but said nothing and nobody noticed him. Only the camera-man who was used to all sorts of things and had had no signal to stop went grinding on recording the whole thing.

The unexpectedness of her onslaught startled the villain off his guard, and the blinding blows that her strong young arm gave were so vigorous and effective that he staggered backward, this way and that, dodging, guarding, acting like a very coward before the vengeance of her righteous wrath. She dealt a blow between his eyes that sent a sharp pain darting through his brain and followed it with another that almost sent him to the floor. He nearly tumbled over a chair in his haste to get away.

Little by little in the fury of her young might she drove him to the wall out at the door and closed and locked it as was planned, but not for any planning did she do it. It was all very real to her. She had seen the slimy soul of the man as it looked forth at her through the flickering candle-light, and her pure soul had gone to war with it and vanquished it from sight. Now as she turned back to the room she stood with trembling body all unnerved, her face grown white and haggard in the flare of the candle blaze, and lifting up her arms and her white face to heaven in one pleading cry, "O God! help me!" she dropped in a little shuddering heap beside the couch, her long hair falling about her, and sobbed out her heart's trouble.

It was a wonderful picture with the flare of light over all. There never had been such a wonderful picture caught before by that company. They hardly dared believe it was theirs, or that the prize of this star actor had really come to them.

Silently Farley lifted up his hand as a signal to shut off the machine. Quietly he motioned the rest of the company to go away and leave them, and then he and Bob stood and faced one another.

"What did I tell you? asked the eyes of Farley, though he spoke no word.

"Well, you've got one on me at last!" growled Bob, "but guess you've done your last film with her. Look at her. That wasn't acting, that was real. She'll never forgive that!"

When Gail went down to the office a few minutes later there was nobody there but Farley, and he turned around pleasantly. "I hope you didn't misunderstand our Mr. Charmer, Miss," he said apologetically. "He's been used to doing acts in a diff'runt class of films than ours, and he gets a little fresh now and then. He didn't mean nothing personal of course, and he wants training. But I gues he'll understand all right after this, and I got you to thank fer givin' him one good lesson. He wanted me to tell you he was sorry he'd made you think he done things wrong. He admires your nerve, and he respects you, and he wants a chance to apologize. I must say you done him up rare."

Gail's white face set visibly. She had not recovered from the shock of what had passed. She felt utterly disgraced, and she was certain he was lying about Charmer. The man saw it and hastened on with his remarks.

"I'm goin' to pay you five dollars extra for today's work,

Miss. You done better than I had any idee you could without havin' no experience before."

The man held out the money smiling.

"You needn't feel shy 'bout takin' it," he said jovially. "You earned it all right. You sure did good solid work. Some o' them other girls are so flighty we have to do a scene all over again every little while; but you went straight through with things and never hindered us a bit ner fussed like they do, ner complained neither. I do like folks not to complain. It makes things go a lot easier, don't you think so? Now, about tomorrow——"

Gail held up her hand.

"Mr. Farley, I can't come tomorrow. I could never go through a scene like that again, not if I starved."

"Oh, now looka here, Miss—what d'you say your name was? Desmond? Oh, yes, now I remember. Now looka here, Miss Desmond, you mustn't talk like that. Why, you don't know how you done up Archie. Why, he's just plain laid out, he was, when he came down here. He says, 'Mist' Fahley,' he says, 'I've just cooked my cake, I have. That girl'll always think I'm a real villain, she will, an' there ain't nothin' can turn her from it,' he says. 'I can't hold up my head no more as an actor. I'm done for.' " The man Farley was good at making up a story as he went along. " 'To have a girl like that lay me out that way through a misunderstanding is too much,' he says; 'an' such a girl!' he says. 'You can see she's the real thing!' he says, 'been used to havin' real high-up attention,' he says; 'been used to gentlemen!' he says, 'an' I can't act no more till I know she's forgive me, an' I want you should tell her what I said.'

"And I says, 'Well, Archie, I think you was pretty fresh myself. From where I stood I could see you was, and I been tellin' you right along that you couldn't carry a line like that in our comp'ny, b'cause we always deal in refined films. We ain't never manufactured anything else but refined films. You can ask the National Censorship Committee if that ain't true. They've never took up no case against us, not one! We got that reputation an' we gotta live up to it. We can't afford to get no sucha name by havin' unrefined acts. We gotta be on the safe side, Archie,' I says, 'an' ef you can't tone yourself down to suit the place, why then the place's vacant for you, Archie, that's all. You gotcher lesson. Now learn it!"

"An' Archie, he says, 'I'll learn it, I will, all right after this. That girl learned me a lot this afternoon, she did. I see things from a diff'runt standpoint now that I never see before,' he says, 'an' I'm a-goin' to ac' diff'runt after this.' An' so I says, 'Well, I'll tell her Archie, but I can't say how she'll take it. She's pretty much up in the air, I can see, an' I ain't to blame if she's so sore about it she turns you down. You better speak to her yourself!' I says."

"That isn't at all necessary," said Gail, speaking up quickly and coldly. "Just tell Mr. Charmer that I accept his apology. But I can't think of continuing in the position any longer. I'll keep the money that I earned today, but I don't want any more."

"Now, Miss Desmond, looka here!" said Farley, "I ain't gonna take no fer an answer! Not specially when you underwent annoyance in our employ. You think I'm a-gonta lose a good high-class actress like you are fer any fresh fella like Arch Charmer? Ef you can't give Arch Charmer another chance, then he goes. I've said it an' I'll stick to it. Archie's fate lies in your fair hand, Miss Desmond. If it comes to a choice between you an' him, I take you every time. I'm willin' to pay you ten dollars a day an' use only high-class stuff. In fact, you can jest about pick yer own plays, if you like. There you have a chance to do a little real philanthropic good in the world. Help me elevate the masses through the movin' pictures. There isn't anything so educatin' in the world and I'm doin' a thankless job all by myself. Bob's helpin' me some, I'll admit, but Bob can't see it yet. Bob thinks it won't pay. He says to me, 'Harry!' says he, 'people don't want to be uplifted. They won't pay fer it, and we can't afford to give it to 'em. We can't afford to get good actors to act refined plays.' Why, Bob even said we couldn't keep you. He said you were too refined for the rest of the comp'ny. He said that yesterday when I hired you!"

Mr. Farley had been a drummer for ladies' silk hosiery before he took up the moving-picture business, and his tongue was long and agile. He had started in to talk the new girl into staying, and he meant to do it. He saw possibilities in her that his business training told him were of great commercial value. So he talked, watching her face and changing his arguments with every varying expression.

Gail was tired to desperation. She was almost sick with excitement and fatigue and the feeling of disgrace that was upon her. But the man rattled on, fondly supposing that his arguments were bringing her to a different view of things. Suddenly she broke in upon his harrangue with a question.

"Mr. Farley, what about that scene? Can you leave it out entirely? Because I couldn't consent to go through it again with that man or any other, no matter how they did it."

"Sure!" lied Farley soothingly. "Sure we can let that go. Cut it here and there or leave it out entirely. We couldn't think of putting you through that again after all you've went through already about it. Not that you would be troubled that way again. Poor Archie will be a humble one from now on, I can tell you, but I wouldn't ask it of you. In fact the rest of the play is so good we can afford to cut a little. Often have to do that. It's all in the day's work, you know."

He smiled affably and again held out the five dollars. He was reasonably sure he had won her over.

"You needn't come in early tomorrow morning; just take a good rest. Make it ten o'clock. That'll suit all right. We—"

Gail stopped him.

"Mr. Farley, I thank you for your kind offer, but it is utterly impossible for me to continue in this work. This afternoon's experience has opened my eyes and made me realize what I have done in allowing myself through want of money to get into it at all. I am not a fool, and I realize that such scenes as that one this afternoon are common on the stage. But the actors who go through with them must throw away their principles, and I cannot do that. I have done wrong in taking the position at all. I cannot think of remaining. Not if you offered me a thousand dollars a day. God will take care of me. Good-bye, Mr. Farley."

She was gone, leaving the nonplused man staring after her in utter amazement, his money still in his hand. What kind of a girl could this be? He had flattered himself that he had recognized that she was different from most girls, but what a strange way of talking. What did she mean by "God will take care of me"? Could she mean that she was willing to take a chance on God's giving her food and clothes? Well, she must be crazy. He shrugged his shoulders and turned back to his desk. They had the film anyway, and they must get it released at the first possible minute or there was no telling what strange thing might happen next. He thought he had made a wonderful find, right on the street, as it were. She had helped them to make the best picture the firm ever had produced, and now she had balked, all on account of that fool Charmer and a funny notion about God. Well it was a strange world. He must see to it that Charmer apologized the next day himself; maybe that would do.

Now it was up to him to see that that film was released as soon as possible.

Gail was as one in a dream as she stumbled back to her room. She wanted nothing so much as to be alone. She was not clear in her mind about anything except that this awful experience that had come to her was of her own doing. She remembered how she had rushed out the day before—was it only the day before?—without even so much as a hurried prayer for guidance. Oh, how could she have forgotten? She flung herself upon the bed and cried as she had not cried since she was a little child.

Late the next afternoon the clerk in the office downstairs

looked up to see one of the regular roomers excitedly hurrying toward her.

"Miss Rittenhouse, I'm sure something is wrong in the room next to mine. I heard someone moaning this morning before I left, and now I hear it again. Is someone sick there?"

"I'm sure I don't know, unless it's that forsaken-looking girl in the dark-blue dress. I've thought she would get pneumonia the way she runs around in the rain in that thin little coat."

The two women hurried up to see, and after getting no response to a knock the clerk opened the door with her passkey.

17

GAIL was kneeling by the bed moaning and calling like a little child, "Father! Father! forgive me!"

They lifted her into bed and the clerk hurried down to call a doctor.

"I hope it's nothing contagious," she fretted, "or we'll all be put in quarantine."

The other woman worked awkwardly at Gail's clothes, trying to make her more comfortable. She was not used to sickness and had no idea how to deal with it.

When the brisk young doctor came he looked with interest and gentle pity at the weary lines on the sweet young face. After his examination he held a consulation with the two women.

"She ought to go to a hospital at once, if she is to live," he said. "Where are her friends?"

"I doubt if she has any," Miss Rittenhouse answered, a worried pucker between her brows. "She didn't give any home address when she registered. She has been hunting a job for weeks. I don't know whether she has found one yet or not."

"Here's three dollars and some change in her purse." The

other woman had been looking in Gail's bag for some mark of identification.

"Very likely that's all she has then, for she has been thinner and more worried every time she went through the office."

"Poor little girl," sighed the doctor. "Well, I'll have to take her to the ward. I doubt if she has strength enough to pull through at all. Call the hospital if you find she has friends or relatives. I'll send the ambulance right down."

The young doctor glanced again at the beautiful lashes drooping sadly over the flushed cheeks and hurried away to his next case.

Not many minutes after the last clang of the ambulance bell had died away in the distance, Miss Rittenhouse looked up to see a handsome young man enter the lobby. One could tell on close examination that his somewhat startling complexion was carefully put on. He brushed a little fleck of lint from his coat as he walked toward the desk.

"Miss Desmond?" He enunciated with the slightest upward inflection as if to admit unwillingly that he really was asking a question. He daintily extracted a card from his pocket. "Mr. Charmer calling," he murmured as though the information were quite unnecessary and as though the call itself were an honor to the whole building.

The usually stern and unbending Miss Rittenhouse suddenly melted. She did not attend the movies for nothing, although she did go to the early show so as to be fresh for her work, for at her age a position must not be thrown away lightly. The visitor was quite familiar to her and her eyes lighted.

"Oh, Mr. Charmer! Archie Charmer, of course!" she murmured to herself in honeyed tones. She took the card as though it were marked "Handle with care." But Mr. Charmer was accustomed to such receptions. He repeated his errand.

"Is Miss Desmond in?"

Miss Rittenhouse's face fell. To think that she should meet this wonderful hero and be obliged to disappoint him! What could he want of that common looking girl?

"I'm so sorry! Miss Desmond was taken to the hospital just now. She is very ill." Miss Rittenhouse seemed to apologize in her tone for Gail's error in being sick when he called.

Amazement showed in every line of the actor's well-tailored figure.

"Why—why—you don't say! I just saw her yesterday. She seemed strong enough then." He ruefully rubbed his cheek where, even through his careful make-up, there showed bruises of various colors.

"She is very, very sick, the doctor said. Is there any message you care to leave?"

Mr. Charmer had been given to understand that it was as much as his position was worth not to bring back Miss Desmond to the employ of the company. So much against his own desires he felt that he must follow her. After the wild attacks upon him yesterday visions of himself calling at an insane asylum suggested themselves. But he was reassured when Miss Rittenhouse told him that Gail had pneumonia and named the hospital to which she had been taken.

Miss Rittenhouse followed him out with adoring eyes and watched him far down the street. Romance was coming her way at last. Today had been full of the unexpected. She went back to her desk wishing that she had been the one for whom the worried look had come into the eyes of the moving-picture hero.

Before long a huge bunch of roses stood beside the bed of the pneumonia patient in the ward. They bore the card of Mr. Archie Charmer, but they had been bought with the company's money after much and stormy discussion between Farley and Bob with Charmer, for business reasons, on neutral ground.

A humbly expressed wish had been dictated by Farley that Miss Desmond would have a rapid recovery. But the flowers stood unnoticed except by the other patients, who welcomed them with delight, and the card was not read. Gail tossed and moaned, unheeding.

Benedict got in the New York sleeper and threw himself full length upon the couch in the state-room. He was weary unto death. This was the third time he had been called to New York since the night he had hurried off leaving Dorothy and her delighted betrothed in his office. It was always to follow up a faint clue that the detective had got wind of, this time a girl who had gone as a nursery governess with a woman from Washington. She was reported to have left Washington the day that Gail must have reached there.

He was taking as much pains about it as if he were sure it was the right trail he was following, but in his heart he knew he had lost hope. He had a feeling that all people get who have made mistakes, that he was being punished for his past follies and that nothing happy would ever come his way again. He had been saved from the sea for what? This? Would his life ever be worth anything again if he did not find Gail? Why, oh why had he not told her of his love before he went away from her? Why had she not waited for him? Dorothy Stanford now represented to him all the mistakes of his past life that had clung about him and tried to drag him down from his ideal. His heart was torn with remorse.

His fitful sleep gave him no real rest. He was continually waking in distress from dreams in which Dorothy contended with Gail for his soul, which seemed a helpless thing and lay on the ground with broken wings unable to soar up to God.

In the morning he went to a hotel, made himself ready for his task, and set forth to find the address given him by the detective.

He had to wait nearly an hour in a miserable little servant's dining-room for the young woman he sought to come downstairs, and while he waited his blood boiled to think what ignominy the royal girl he loved might be enduring while she earned her living. He looked around on the cheerless place and listened to the clanging voices of the servants in the kitchen, and grew more sick of soul.

At last she came, a little tired creature with sad eyes circled darkly, and a drooping pathetic little mouth. She explained that she could not leave a naughty child until its mother came, and she looked wearily perplexed to know why he had come.

"Are you the young woman who came from Washington with Mrs. V. S. Barker?" he asked, rising deferentially.

"I am."

"The one who came to be governess to some children, and had come into Washington from the shore only the day before?"

"I am," she said, and her tone was slightly resentful, as if she questioned his right to make all these inquiries.

"Then I must ask your pardon for annoying you," he said sadly. "You are not the one I am looking for. I am in search of a dear friend whose whereabouts I do not know, but who came to Washington on that same day in search of a position. I thought I had traced her here. Her name is Miss Desmond."

The girl sadly shook her head. There was something wistful about her eyes, as if she wished she were the one that splendid-looking man was searching for and that he would take her away from the grind and loneliness of her unpleasant position.

"There's no such person here," she said; "and I'm sure if you care anything about her you may be glad she didn't find this place. It's no bed of roses, I can tell you." There was something sharp and hard about her young voice in its pain. He wished he might do something to make things happier for her, but of course he couldn't.

"I'm sorry," he said pleasantly, "both for myself and for you. If Miss Desmond were here she would not be here long, for I should take her away. I hope you will pardon my intrusion, and I hope things may brighten up for you."

She thanked him and wistfully watched him go away, but her mood clung about him and depressed him. He felt as if his body were too heavy to carry, and each foot was like lead as he lifted it. What a world of sadness and disappointment it was! Why did it have to be? He wished he might do something to help lift the gloom, but how could one go about it? Gail would know. Gail was sunshine and strength in herself. Why was she created the only woman who knew the secret of a beautiful life? Of course there might be others, but they had not come into his life. If he could but find her! Yet how hopeless it seemed now that he ever would! The world stretched out an endless haystack in which he was searching for the proverbial tiny needle. He had searched so long in vain. Where were his prayers? Ah, he was no pray-er. Probably they were not acceptable to the Most High. Look at the life he had lived, selfish, indulgent. How could he expect anything from God? He knew from the reading that he had already done in the Book that it was the righteous man whose prayers availed much. He had lived for the pleasure of the hour. Why should God answer him?

And yet, the quiet voice at the evening-time in the still sweet room by the sea had said: "If ye abide in me, and my words abide in you, ye shall ask what ye will and it shall be done unto you."

Well, so far as he knew how he was trying to abide, and to find out the words and let them be in his heart for a guide. But he had prayed and prayed and it had done no good. Yet even as he thought this, his heart was sending forth another anguished cry: "O God, let me find her! O God, let me find her! Keep her safely and let me find her!"

He was walking on and on, he knew not whither. It was Broadway, where traffic was crowded. He supposed the next thing to do would be to return to Washington. This trip had been a useless thing as all other efforts had proved.

He shivered with the cold wind that blew upon him. The

day was dark and heavy clouds were scudding overhead like black ships on hasty evil business. Great splashes of rain suddenly dashed down and struck him in the face like hailstones. A gust of wind swept up the street and took people's hats from their heads. The river and ocean seemed to have risen from their beds and entered the city, taking possession of the atmosphere. People with umbrellas opened them and closed them as suddenly lest they turn inside out or vanish from their sight. Something seemed to break in the skies and a torrent was let loose without warning. Everybody dashed into doorways and crowded against one another to get out of the tempest.

Benedict with the rest backed into an entryway or vestibule in front of a moving-picture theater. A bill-board blew down and just missed striking him as it fell. Women dashed past him to the most sheltered spots, for the rain was driving straight in as if it were chasing its victims. The girl in the ticket stand looked as if she were a mermaid under a fountain, so quickly was her glass case covered with raindrops. People were slinging out nickels and dimes and snatching blue and pink tickets and pushing their way to the door. A burst of uproarious music floated out in jerks each time a new person entered. Benedict saw that it was the only refuge available and that might soon be gone, for the seats would all be filled. He put down some money, snatched his ticket with the rest, and plunged toward the door.

In due time he reached it, the back of his neck and shoulders wet from the storm, and standing in the crowded darkness waiting for the usher to take him to a seat his eyes naturally sought the only lighted spot in the room, the living, brilliant screen.

A man was stepping into view as if he had just come out on the platform unexpectedly and was looking about impudently on the audience. A man with coarse handsome features and a dissipated look. There was nothing about him to attract a man like Benedict, and all to repel, and yet his gaze was held. The man on the screen leered about, smiled contemptuously, and winked insolently, took out a cigarette and lighted it; smoked and laughed again. Benedict experienced an intense dislike for him and was glad when he walked away with a flippant wave of his hand and another insolent smile.

Two pert, painted girls attired with a view to economy of material and a studied atmosphere of the grotesque about the arrangement of their coiffures, came now in turn and looked at the audience with bold knowing glances, and mocking smiles upon their painted lips. They lingered like an ugly thought, but the last was turning to go as an usher came and put him in a seat. An old woman in kitchen garb and soiled face with stringy hair made her fleeting bow, and when he looked up again as he dropped into his seat wearily a girl stood there that made his heart stand still with wonder.

It was Gail, her very self, looking from an open window framed in roses, looking far and wistfully as he had seen her look beside the sea; bringing her eyes back and focusing them gravely, earnestly upon the audience, upon his face, yet not as if she knew him, and looking far again. She turned her head away to look behind her, then back with a sad little tender smile as if she missed something and could not find it. Once her hand went swiftly to her throat and she drew a deep breath as if a heavy burden were upon her that she was bearing bravely. Then she turned back and smiled again, a cheerful little forced smile that would not intrude its troubles upon strangers. Then came that faraway look—that searching of the sea, shading her eyes as if the light hurt them. She turned slightly more toward the audience again and looked them in the eyes with a grave quiet dignity that sat upon her sweet face graciously and so smiling, with a slight inclination of her head she turned and faded into shadow.

The man in the seat next to Benedict turned and looked at him curiously, his breath came so heavily. He wondered if this stranger whose sleeves were wet where his hand had touched them, was going into a fit of apoplexy, or if he had the asthma? But Benedict did not notice his curious look. He was with difficulty restraining himself from rushing down the aisle after the vision of his dreams before she went away. He had just sense enough left to know that she was a picture and that if he waited he might possibly see her again.

When he first sank into the seat he had meant to put his head back and shut his eyes and rest. But now he was all alive to the screen and what would happen next. His breath came fast, and the perspiration stood in beads on his forehead. He clenched the arms of the seat with his hands as if his life depended on it, and watched with strained intensity while the first scene passed without her coming. He had nearly persuaded himself that it could not be Gail herself, but some girl who looked strangely like her.

Presently she came walking rapidly down a city street, looking from side to side at the signs, and pausing anxiously before an employment office. She turned as she went in the door and looked toward the front with that little troubled pucker in her brow that he had noticed some times when he had not felt so well as usual. He read worry in her eyes. He knew by instinct what trouble she was having finding a job. It was all very real to him. His thoughts had pictured some fears for her like this. He could not doubt it had been true. Once or twice he even began to think it was all a hallucination, and rubbing his eyes, looked about on the audience wondering. Were they seeing the same scenes that he thought he saw or had his brain begun to see strange fancies? Was it Gail, indeed, or only someone who looked like her? No, there was the same little dark blue gown she had worn with the white frills at her wrists and neck. He had taken that very sleeve between his thumb and finger once when she sat by his side just because he loved to touch anything that belonged to her. No, there could be no doubt but that the original was Gail, unless his eyes were playing false. He suddenly reached out and touched the man by his side.

"Say, will you tell me, has that girl got little white ruffles on a dark dress, and is she the same one who came out last in the beginning? I'm a little mixed up."

The stranger edged away. He evidently thought his neighbor was a bit crazy, but he answered:

"Yes, yes, that's her. She's got some white ruffle things on her dress. Yes, that's the last one that come out. She's huntin' a job you know. Up against it like, I reckon."

"I see! Thank you," said Benedict, and sat back more calmly. Then he was looking at a real picture unless, indeed, the man and the audience and everything were fantasies. In that case what did it matter? Maybe he was not real himself.

His brain whirled on in a million strange ideas, while his heart was wrung with anguish over the trials of the girl before him. That it was merely acting never really occurred to him while it was going on. His heart knew it must have been true or she never could have looked that way. He walked the pictured streets and went into the pictured houses and offices with her searching for a position, and lived and breathed beside her, agonizing that he could not reach out and draw her to him away from all this trouble into the quiet of his love and protection.

The scenes reeled rapidly on unfolding the story bit by bit till it came to that fatal scene where the villain entered her room during her absence and hid behind the screen just as she entered her door with the candle. Benedict gripped the arms of the seat anew, and almost sprang up. It seemed that he must go down there and haul that villain out of his hiding-place and beat the life out of him. He must protect the girl he loved somehow. His breath came so hard again that the man beside him got up and pushed past murmuring something about going down nearer to an empty seat where he could see better. But Benedict did not notice. He was holding himself by mainforce from springing up and running down the aisle. He kept saying to himself, "That is only a picture. Whatever happened has happened already, and that beast of a man is not really there at all. I must find out where he is and how to get after him."

Over and over he told himself that and tried to keep calm, but when she stood there looking about with the candle light on her sweet tired face, his heart thrilled to go to her. When she fell asleep and the villain stole softly toward her with the evil smirk on his face, the young man uttered a low threatening sound in his throat and clenched his fists in the dark, his whole strong body trembling with anger and horror.

With body tense and eyes straining through the dark he leaned forward as though about to spring when the wretch drew close to the sleeping girl. And then she turned and lifted up that frightened terrified glance, her long hair falling away from her face, her eyes lighting with alarm. She sprang at the man.

Not only Benedict but the whole audience broke forth into a soft murmur of approval after a breathless moment, and the picture moved on to its finish amid a silence that seldom comes in any audience. Perhaps in all New York there was not a record so amazing as that unconscious acting that Gail Desmond in her real horror and agony had done that first day of her engagement as a moving-picture actress. The audience went fairly wild when she at last vanquished the villain and locked her door upon him. But when she turned and lifted up her hands with the agony still in her white face and prayed her frantic little prayer, and then fell upon her knees beside the couch and shook with sobs, the man in the audience who loved her bowed his head upon his hands and groaned, "O God, help her!"

Some people near him turned and looked back curiously, then smiled and shrugged their shoulders. They thought he must be drunk. But Benedict lifted his head and watched the picture again to the end, unconscious of the curious smiles.

Not until the story was finished, the villain finally set in his right place, and the girl gone on her way unharmed did he relax his tension and begin to think. The play came to an end abruptly and a foolish slap-stick act of tricks and juggled farces followed which whirled before his eyes and mind like motes upon a beam of sunshine. He saw nothing more. He had set himself to think what he should do.

He was not a frequenter of moving-picture shows, but he had been enough to know that if he stayed there long enough this play would be repeated and he should again look upon the face he had searched so long to find. His hungry heart cried out against waiting while processions of endless soldiers marched over reeling streets, and crowds of people swarmed to see some notable who passed. Monkeys learned to spell their names, flowers unfolded before his eyes from buds into full-blown roses, or some family living in the seventh story of an apartment house fell successively through the several ceilings to the street and had to run away pursued by all the inhabitants of the land on foot and in automobiles. The whole was one terrible jumble.

It gradually dawned upon him that he might find out the name of this play when it came on again, and so he watched each separate part till the hour rolled by and the villain stepped forth into the arena once more and smiled his brutish smile. Benedict shut his teeth hard and thrilled to think how his strong sweet girl had held this beast at bay. Somewhere that man lived and breathed upon this earth and menaced womankind. He felt instinctively as Gail had done that the beast he had acted was his natural self, and that was why he had done it so well. Somewhere he would find him and deal him out the punishment he deserved, and put him where he could not do any harm. He had two people now to find, Gail and the man who had dared to look at her even in a picture as this man had done.

Carefully he studied the names at the beginning. "Released by the Ray-See Film Company." He must remember that. He shivered at the thought of Gail's being connected with such a company as that. Where would he find the Ray-See Film Company? Would they be in the telephone-book? Would the men in charge of the theater know? How soon could he discover them? Were they located here or in some Western state, possibly in Hollywood? Would it be long before he found them? And when he had found them, would she be with them still or would she have drifted away again? Oh, the long, awful strain with its endless vistas of anguish that stretched ahead!

18

WHEN the picture was finished the second time, Benedict arose and went to interview the doorkeeper. Yes, "A Woman's Hand" was a "Ray-See" film. Yes, they had an office somewhere in the city he thought. He would better ask the manager. He'd be in that afternoon about three.

Benedict thanked the man and went out. He did not intend to wait until three o'clock to find out about Gail if he could help it.

He sought the nearest telephone and looked through the book. Yes, there was the Ray-See Film Company. It almost seemed too good to be true. He looked at it hard as if it might vanish from his gaze if he did not fix it thoroughly in his brain. He took out his pen and wrote down the address, and then went out and took a taxi to the door.

The young woman with the abbreviated dress and the plastered hair was in her place pounding away at the typewriter and keeping time with her jaws and a liberal portion of gum. She stopped and looked up alertly when the exceedingly interesting young man in the unmistakably fine raiment entered the door and inquired for the manager.

She arose and came forward with a smile, her jaws suspending operations for the purpose, her round baby eyes fastened upon him with admiration.

"You want Mistah Fahley? Well, I'm real sorry, but he's out of town. He went off with the comp'ny yest'iddy. They've went up state to do a lot of special stuff an' he thought he hadta go along. Bob's here. You like to see Bob? He'll be in presently. Bob's next thing to Mistah Fahley. He's outta lunch. Guess he'll be in about one ur half past. Could I give him a message, ur will you wait?"

Benedict drew a troubled sigh. There it was again, wait, wait, wait! How could he wait another minute?

"Why, I don't know," he said, hesitating. "I wanted to inquire about a film; that is, I wanted to know something about it. I don't suppose you would know? I'm in a good deal of hurry."

"Sure! I know all about the fillums," giggled the girl. "Ain't much goes on here I don't know. What you want to do? Rent? Ur buy it? I could tend to that for you. That's what I'm here for. I don't do much else except write letters."

"Why, no; I didn't want to get a film at all. I merely wanted to inquire about one of the—the—that is, one of the ladies who appears in one of the films. She strongly resembles a friend of mine of whom I have lost sight, and I was wondering if I could trace her whereabouts. I saw this film this morning on Broadway while I took refuge from the rain."

It seemed almost necessary to his dignity as Gail's friend and protector that he explain to this exceedingly fresh young person why he happened to be going to a Broadway movie in the morning. But he need not have taken the trouble. This romantic child of a New York tenement was on fire with interest at once, and she positively could not appreciate his apology.

"What was the play," she asked eagerly, " 'The Glad Hand'?"

"No, 'A Woman's Hand,' " he confessed awkwardly.

"Oh, yes; that!" The girl's eyes narrowed excitedly. "Say, that's some play, ain't it? It's made a great hit, that has. Say, ain't that girl got lovely hair, that one where she beats up Archie Charmer? It's real too, every hair of it. I seen it the day she first come in to apply fer my p'sition, an' me not in it half an' hour. My, wasn't that good luck for me! But I felt punk when I saw how disappointed she was. She sure was up against it. And she was a girl that wasn't used to life. She took it hard, I could see. But Mistah Fahley took her all in with bells on the minnit he laid eyes on her, an' he put her inta that job. She's awful nice, but she's a reg'lar stiff. She ain't no baby-doll, but she can act.

"She raised Cain here in the comp'ny 'count o' her kind o' starrin' in that picture. Flossie Foss was so sore she almost quit. But say, which lady was it you wanted to find? Was it Kittie Cresco, ur Flossie Foss? I bet it's Kittie. She's got friends all over this globe. She's traveled a lot, an' she's awful popular. Did you take notice to the name on the 'nouncement? You didn't? Yes, they always have the names of the actors on our fillums, and they always have 'em out fron the the bills too. Well, was she awful delicate lookin', with a lot of gold hair all flyin' like silk around her face? That's Flossie. Ur did she have long curls like Mary Pickford? That's Kittie. Kittie, she looks an awful lot like Mary Pickford an' she's proud of it. She makes money on that likeness an' takes lots of airs. It wasn't either of them?

"Well, say, you couldn't possibly mean the lady with the hair, could you? Her name's Gail Desmond; swell name, ain't it? But she's one of these regular high-brows. You couldn't touch her 'nless you was an angel, and you couldn't speak to her 'thout knock-down. Say, yo'd oughtta see her do up Archie Charmer. You saw that fillum? Well, that scene was just like it is in the picture. B'lieve me it was real! I was up there an' seen it all standin' just outside the stoodio door. Bob put me onto it that there was gonta be somethin' doin'. Good night! You oughtta seen it.

"You see she didn't know what was comin'. They just told her a little, and they knew her kind wouldn't stand fer Archie, so they turned him loose 'thout tellin' her an' she fought fer her life. Good night! That was some fillum! Didn't you think it was dandy? It's gonta hav' a long run on Broadway, I bet. It's just out.

"But say, she don't know that picture's in. You mustn't tell her. Mistah Fahley would fire me fer tellin' you. You won't gimme away, will you? No sir, she don't know that scene's in at all. She thinks the whole thing's cut. He knowed she wouldn't stand fer it a minnit. He's awful anxious to get her back. He thinks she's somethin' great. He says you can't get that there real natural actin' like she does every day, an' he's willin' to pay her a big salary."

The girl was chattering on, saying anything to detain the handsome young man. What mattered it that her letters were waiting and her overseer would soon be coming back? She didn't get a chance at a man like this one every day.

But the young man was thinking, and at the last sentence as she came to a pause he asked pleasantly:

"Do you happen to know where she is now? Is she working with your company?"

"Oh, no; she left as soon as 'A Woman's Hand' was finished. I heard her tell Mistah Fahley that she wouldn't come back if he gave her a thousand dollars a day. You see, he thought I wasn't there, but I hadn't gone home yet; I sensed there was goin' to be fireworks and I wanted to be in on 'em. She certainly did tell him what she thought of Archie Charmer, and the whole company in general. An' just after he offered her double pay, she quit on him cold an' sailed out of the office like a queen an' left him starin'. Whaddya think o' that? My stars! If I'd the chance she had I'd have snapped at it, b'lieve me. But I can see her point an' a girl like her don't belong with this gang anyway. She oughta get a job as a swell governess or, what's better, she oughtn't to hafta work fer her livin' at all. She's kinda frail and she oughta be taken care of. I'm real fond o' that girl, though some o' the comp'ny couldn't see her at all. They was all sore at the way she treated Arch Charmer, an' then besides, she was way beyond them anyway you look at it."

Benedict began to beam. Here was one after his own heart. Surely he could get some valuable aid from her, if he could ever stop her talking long enough to make her answer his questions.

"I feel exactly as you do about Miss Desmond, Miss— er—"

"Dodd's my name. Terrible, ain't it?"

"Miss Dodd," went on Benedict, ignoring her remark, "I think you are right in your opinion of Miss Desmond. She is a girl in a million and should be taken care of. That is why I have come. I want to find her."

As Benedict took her into his confidence Miss Dodd's floured face began to light up. Here, indeed was a fitting climax to the romantic scenes that had been occurring in the office since the memorable day when Miss Desmond stepped in and that memorable play of "A Woman's Hand" had been filmed. It was right and according to all the rules of romance that a hero should be found for the lovely young actress who had been pursued by the villain in the play.

"My stars! You don't mean it! No kiddin', are you really goin' to marry her? Say now, ain't that great! Well, she certainly needs you right now, I guess. She's at the hospital with a bad case of pneumonia and I don't know whether they think she's gonta live ur not. Here's the address. Arch Charmer left it layin' around and I thought I might need it sometime. Good-bye and good luck to ya. Let me know how she is, if yah get a chance."

At the news Benedict's heart felt as if an icy hand clutched it, and with hurried but sincere thanks to the kind-hearted girl who had helped him, he shook her hand in a grip like iron and hastened away.

In the taxicab Benedict found himself praying over and over again, "O God! save her! save her!" and he added the new prayer which he had learned in the last weeks after faithful study, in his new Bible and many long nights spent in agonized struggle on his knees: "Thy will be done."

In the hospital the brisk young doctor welcomed him with grave relief, looking him over with satisfaction that at last the lovely patient had a friend, and one who seemed in every way right for her.

"Come this way," he said. "We have moved her from the ward to this private room. It was empty and she needed the quiet."

Benedict followed, cut to the heart to think that his beloved one should have to suffer in such a place when he had the finest of everything in his illness, thanks to her loving sacrifice.

As he looked again on the sweet face motionless on the pillow he almost gave way, for his nerves had been strained to the utmost. He knelt beside the bed and hid his face that the doctor might not see what he felt. But his soul was in his eyes as he looked up again, hungry for a glance of recognition from the dear face on the pillow.

The doctor gently motioned him away. In the hall they had a long talk. Two special nurses were installed, one for day and one for night duty, for the dreaded crisis would be passed that night. Everything possible to be done for the patient was arranged for. Benedict sent a telegram to Mrs. Battin to let the two loving hearts know that the search was over. And then he set himself to wait and pray.

It was not until long after midnight that the doctor touched Benedict on the shoulder and with a smile gave him the glad news that Gail had come through safely. He sent the exhausted young man to a near-by hotel and bade him sleep as long as he could. In the morning he might come into the patient's room again for one glimpse of her. It might be that she would know him.

With a heart overflowing with thankfulness and eagerness

for the morrow, Benedict almost ran to his hotel, sending another telegram on his way upstairs, to ease the hearts of the anxious women.

As he lay down to sleep the noise of the traffic outside seemed to sing a tune like a lullaby.

> *"I've found her at last. Thank God, I have found her.*
> *I'm going to see her and tell her my love."*

He fell asleep with the words chanting sweet in his heart.

The nurse met him with a smile the next day. She was pleased that her lovely patient belonged to this distinguished-looking man.

As Benedict knelt again beside her, Gail slowly opened her eyes. Bewildered, they rested upon him and then she smiled. And in the glory of her smile was the reflection of all the happy days they had spent together beside the sea. As she closed her eyes again, too weary still to hold them upon him, her lover buried his head in his arms beside her.

Only a moment they let him stay, but he went out into the early spring sunshine as if he were walking on clouds. Did that smile mean that she really cared? Should he dare to go now and buy her a ring? So happy and carefree he was that, almost without his volition, his feet carried him into Tiffany's. A pure blue diamond he bought her, that reminded him of the blue sea they had watched together. And then in his happy eagerness he joyously picked out a dainty circlet with delicate tracery of orange-blossoms. With these in his pocket he stopped at a florist's shop on the avenue. A new thought had come to him. He would send a thank-offering to the only two people in the city who had been unselfishly interested in his finding Gail. The thin little governess with the sad eyes, and the voluble maiden at the office of the film company. He had a feeling that Gail would like him to do it. Besides, he had more business with the second young lady.

So he selected a wealth of roses, masses of them, pink and

crimson, gold and white. About their stems were laid sweet peas and lilies of the valley in sweet profusion. He did not ask how much they cost, but just picked them out and laid them in the box beside the roses with his own hands. He asked for a card and envelope and wrote: "I have found the way to my friend. Please accept these for the trouble I caused you yesterday. I am very happy and hope you will find a way out of the dark some day."

He signed his name, but slipped a ten-dollar bill into the envelope with the card, sealed it, and tied it to the valley lilies. This box he sent to the governess.

Then he selected a great sheaf of American Beauty roses for the other box, putting in a card with these words:

"For the little girl who helped me find my friend, from Gail Desmond."

He left also an order with the florist for flowers to be delivered daily to the hospital, and with a light heart went on his way.

His next errand was more difficult. He had determined the night before that the picture of his beloved should not be flaunted around the streets of New York, nor any other city. That if it was at all possible he would prevent its being shown again if it took every cent he had.

His interview with "Mistah Fahley" was a long one, but with the skilful aid of the grateful stenographer and after much persuasion and more money, he left the office in triumph, the sole owner of the film and with the surety that it would not be shown anywhere after that week.

That afternoon the doctor let him see Gail again, but still only for a few seconds. It was two whole days before he allowed him to speak to her.

It was a sunny morning and Gail was feeling stronger. She seemed to live only for the little visits he made each day. This morning when Benedict came the nurse felt that it would at last be safe for the patient, if she left them alone together for a little while.

Gail was waiting for him this time, a glorious light in her eyes. Gently, not to frighten her, Benedict sat beside her and pressed his lips to her hand. She feebly returned the clasp, then slowly lifted her hand and put it to her own lips.

"My darling! at last!" Benedict whispered as he drank in the light in her eyes. Gail was too weak to speak, but her look of joy was enough for him, as he gently slipped the beautiful ring on her finger.

The weeks that followed were even more beautiful than those they had spent together by the sea. There were plans to be made and all the events of the terrible weeks of separation to be talked over.

"It was all my fault," said Gail sadly, as they sat together one day in the little sun-parlor of the hospital. "I should never have got into that terrible picture. Honestly I don't know whether I was more frightened that night on the raft than I was when that awful man looked at me in that way. I felt as though I were in the depths of wickedness and there was no way out."

"But no harm came to you, for the Lord was able to bring you out as He brought us out of the depths of the storm. And I have come to realize in these last few weeks that He has brought me out of worse depths than I even dreamed I was in. For now that I know Him I can see how hopeless and unhappy I was without Him. Just today I was reading that 'He raised us up to sit together with Him in heavenly places in Christ Jesus.' It may be that He had to let us go through the depths of death before we would care enough to call to Him to raise us up."

When the days of convalescence were over, a simple little wedding was held in Mrs. Battin's home. Corinne was very much in evidence those days, and when she stood on the porch, her hands on her ample hips, watching the two drive away to spend a week in Mrs. Battin's little cottage at The Point, she turned to her mistress with a puzzling question.

"I d'clare it do beat all, how de good Lord wo'ks. Now

here them two chilluns wouldn't never have known each other ef it hadn't 'a' been fer dat boat accidemp. Now all my life I has prayed, 'O Lord, don't let me neveh have to go on no boats!' Now Mis' Battin,' honey, do you s'pose ef I had 'a' tooken a boat trip de good Lord would have give me a grand man like dat ar?"

About the Author

Grace Livingston Hill is well-known as one of the most prolific writers of romantic fiction. Her personal life was fraught with joys and sorrows not unlike those experienced by many of her fictional heroines.

Born in Wellsville, New York, Grace nearly died during the first hours of life. But her loving parents and friends turned to God in prayer. She survived miraculously, thus her thankful father named her Grace.

Grace was always close to her father, a Presbyterian minister, and her mother, a published writer. It was from them that she learned the art of storytelling. When Grace was twelve, a close aunt surprised her with a hardbound, illustrated copy of one of Grace's stories. This was the beginning of Grace's journey into being a published author.

In 1892 Grace married Fred Hill, a young minister, and they soon had two lovely young daughters. Then came 1901, a difficult year for Grace—the year when, within months of each other, both her father and husband died. Suddenly Grace had to find a new place to live (her home was owned by the church where her husband had been pastor). It was a struggle for Grace to raise her young daughters alone, but through everything she kept writing. In 1902 she produced *The Angel of His Presence, The Story of a Whim,* and *An Unwilling Guest.* In 1903 her two books *According to the Pattern* and *Because of Stephen* were published.

It wasn't long before Grace was a well-known author, but she wanted to go beyond just entertaining her readers. She soon included the message of God's salvation through Jesus Christ in each of her books. For Grace, the most important thing she did was not write books but share the message of salvation, a message she felt God wanted her to share through the abilities he had given her.

In all, Grace Livingston Hill wrote more than one hundred books, all of which have sold thousands of copies and have touched the lives of readers around the world with their message of "enduring love" and the true way to lasting happiness: a relationship with God through his Son, Jesus Christ.

In an interview shortly before her death, Grace's devotion to her Lord still shone clear. She commented that whatever she had accomplished had been God's doing. She was only his servant, one who had tried to follow his teaching in all her thoughts and writing.

Don't miss these Grace Livingston Hill romance novels!

Title	Price
Where Two Ways Meet, Vol. 1	3.95
Bright Arrows, Vol. 2	3.95
A Girl to Come Home To, Vol. 3	3.95
Amorelle, Vol. 4	3.95
Kerry, Vol. 5	4.95
All Through the Night, Vol. 6	4.95
The Best Man, Vol. 7	3.95
Ariel Custer, Vol. 8	3.95
The Girl of the Woods, Vol. 9	3.95
More Than Conqueror, Vol. 11	3.95
Head of the House, Vol. 12	4.95
White Orchids, Vol. 28	3.95
The Ransom, Vol. 77	3.95
Found Treasure, Vol. 78	3.50
The Big Blue Soldier, Vol. 79	3.50
The Challengers, Vol. 80	3.95
Duskin, Vol. 81	4.95
The White Flower, Vol. 82	3.95
Marcia Schuyler, Vol. 83	4.95
Cloudy Jewel, Vol. 84	4.95
Crimson Mountain, Vol. 85	3.95
The Mystery of Mary, Vol. 86	3.50
The Honeymoon House	3.95
The Angel of His Presence	3.95
Katharine's Yesterday	3.95

The Grace Livingston Hill romance novels are available at your local bookstore, or you may order by mail (U.S. and territories only). Send your check or money order plus $1.25 per book ordered for postage and handling to:

Tyndale D.M.S.
Box 80
Wheaton, Illinois 60189

Prices subject to change. Allow 4-6 weeks for delivery.
Tyndale House Publishers, Inc.